THE
VISITORS
RICHARD GANNS

ISBN: 979-8-218-21084-7

Nothing endures but hope.

AT THE TURN of the twenty-third century, humanity has colonized much of our solar system. The emerging Sol System culture, largely independent of Earth, is based on asteroid mining and low-gravity processing and manufacturing. The capital city of Mars, Hawkington, is the hub of government, industry, science and technology, education, and the arts. Humanity has faced and overcome the challenges of colonizing space and the resurrection of a nearly-destroyed home world. But is it prepared for the next challenge?

1

THE SHUTTLE LURCHED, descended to the Ellis Habitat docking port, and connected its boarding hatch. Passengers recovered their stowed bags and queued up to the exit. Logan Rhodes slouched motionless in his seat, his head leaning against the curved cabin wall. The flight attendant gave him a concerned look and then retrieved the two empty drink containers from his seat table.

Logan was not the type to attract attention. Wearing a standard, if shabby, business suit, with combed brown hair, and clean-shaven, he went unnoticed. Some would consider him handsome, but in every sense, Logan was ordinary. The shuttle's low-frequency rumble was soothing beneath the passengers' hushed conversation, and Logan dozed.

The flight attendant announced their arrival at Ellis Habitat, one of many orbitals in Delta Sector. Based on the Stanford Torus design, it provided terrestrial gravity at the habitation level. A controlled biosphere, extensive landscaping, and businesses and residences made Ellis Habitat a desirable destination. A cooperative local government functioned much like an Earth-side municipality.

The flight attendant reminded the passengers to have their ID and itinerary ready for security screening. Now out of his seat,

Logan shouldered his bag and shuffled out the hatch and down the boarding tube into the habitat transport terminal.

Several uniformed agents stood waiting, flanked by a pair of armored grunts holding carbines. Logan took a deep breath and pulled his ID tag from his jacket pocket. An agent checked a display as he scanned Logan's face and ID, then punched a console button and waved Logan through. In the transport area, Logan found an empty auto-cab. Stepping inside, he passed a credit chip over a sensor, entered the address for Zandax corporate headquarters, and the cab sped off.

The cab followed its programmed route through a tangle of gray composite walls and hedged courtyards. Zandax Corporation's building lay in an area of dense vegetation. Logan exited the cab and looked around as it disappeared down the track to its next fare. He walked into the entrance vestibule where a squad of armed men stood watching. Looking straight ahead, he kept a brisk pace into an atrium, where a man stepped in front of him. The man's suit and insignia were not the standard Zandax security uniform, and he wore no ID tag.

"State your name and business."

"I'm Logan Rhodes from New World Consulting. I have a 10:00 am appointment with Albert Salondo in Systems Engineering."

Who the hell are these guys?

He set his pack on the moving scanner and looked around the atrium. The man examined the scanner display, then waved Logan through.

Logan took the elevator to the office level and found Salondo's office. A man in a gray business suit sat at the desk. He was not Salondo. Logan knocked on the doorframe and peered in. The man looked up in surprise.

"I'm Logan Rhodes. I have an appointment with Albert."

The man stiffened.

"Dr. Salondo does not work here anymore. Perhaps I can help." Backing his chair away from the desk, he tapped a stylus against his knee.

Logan saw a wall cam and no nameplate on the desk.

Odd. Al would have contacted me.

"Excuse me, you are ..."

"My name is Vierek."

"Mr. Vierek, where is Albert?"

"Dr. Salondo was involved in work inconsistent with management's interests. He was encouraged to seek employment elsewhere. What exactly is the nature of your relationship to Dr. Salondo?"

Not clear that it's any of your business, but OK.

"He contracted with me for research and analysis. I need to talk to Albert. How do I contact him?"

Vierek eyed Logan for a moment.

"Dr. Salondo did not leave any contact information."

Bullshit. What the hell's going on here?

On the wall cam behind Vierek's desk, a red light began flashing. While Vierek adjusted his earpiece, Logan pulled his comm from a pocket and pressed the ON button. A message appeared:

Logan — I hope this reaches you in time. Don't go to Zandax. Marsh is there, and I think they know what we were planning.

— Al

Vierek stopped listening to his earpiece and looked at Logan.

"Mr. Rhodes, Dr. Salondo contracted with you while he was a Zandax employee, and the Marsh Corporation now owns that contract. We need you to clarify what you were doing for him."

Marsh. I've heard plenty about it and none of it good. Time to leave.

Logan gave Vierek a bland smile.

"I need to use the washroom. Which way is it?"

Vierek held Logan with an unreadable gaze, then pointed.

"That way. Ten meters down the hall."

Watching Logan, he rolled his chair and reached across the desk for his comm.

Logan walked back into the hallway. He looked around, then shouldered his pack and trotted to a stairwell. He took the stairs to a rear exit. Behind him, the sounds of shouts and the stamping of feet filled the stairwell.

BHANUPRIYA OKA REMOVED her training headset and closed her eyes. She stood and stretched, then headed for the exercise compartment. Passengers on the Earth–Mars transport completed at least two hours daily of resistance and cardio exercise. Bhani had a slight but well-developed build, a round, brown face, and large dark eyes. She used a scrunchie to fasten her jet-black hair into a ponytail and went to a vacant exercise station.

A week earlier, she had boarded the transport in Long Beach, California, the first step in her new career. The transport would soon land at Hawkington, the capital city of Mars. Most of the twenty-five passengers were going to R&D, mining, or manufacturing work in Hawkington. Some were bound for orbiting habitats, like Serenity, home to some 50,000 souls.

During the trip, professional or personal projects occupied most of one's time. The lounge was popular for reading, playing games, socializing, and staring at the exterior cam displays. Two weeks of confinement affected passengers differently, but everyone suffered from restlessness, eventually. Bhani had first noticed the intense, muscular young man in the gym. He had dark skin, a military haircut, and a preoccupied expression on his face. She was careful not to stare at the scars on his legs. Later, in the lounge, she took a seat next to him. Catching his eye, she held out her hand.

"I'm Bhanupriya Oka. Just call me Bhani."

He flashed her a brief, tight smile and shook her hand.

"Julio Ortiz."

"Going to 2060RT2?"

"How could you tell?"

"A hunch. Me too, heading to my first proper job, a mining tech. I'm kind of excited. You?"

"Hopeful. I can do without the excitement."

She studied him for a moment. "What did you do before this?"

He looked out the window. "Army."

"Sorry. I didn't mean to be nosy."

He grinned. "Sure you did. Now it's my turn. What did you do before this?"

She shrugged. "School."

"What school?"

"IIT."

"Which is ...?"

"Indian Institute of Technology, in Kharagpur."

He gave her a skeptical look. "And you're just a mining tech?"

"MTS, actually."

"MTS. Member, Technical Staff." He raised an eyebrow. "So you're not just a field tech. I'm impressed."

She rolled her eyes, exhaled, and shrugged.

He gave her an amused look.

"Embarrassed because you're an engineer and not a grunt?"

She shrugged again. "I don't want to make anyone uncomfortable."

"Why would I feel uncomfortable? Are you going to be my boss?"

She shook her head. "I'm a trainee at this point. I won't be anybody's boss."

"So, Bhani, you're smart and well-educated. I'll try not to hold that against you."

"Where were you before the army?"

"Compton, in Southern California. Grew up there. Worked as a part-time mechanic. The army was my first full-time job."

"What was the army like?"

He glanced out the window. "I was lucky to get out in one piece."

"What did you do after the army?"

"Security guard at the Fensky Lewis Corporation. Lousy job. I was glad to get on with Alpha Zubrin."

"Wow. That's quite a path. Have you done this sort of mining work before?"

"No. We're both newbies."

"I have a proposal. I won't laugh at your screw-ups if you don't laugh at mine."

He sipped his drink. "Counter proposal: you laugh at mine because I'll be laughing at yours."

THE MARSH CORPORATION had assigned Bruce Spencer to run the security department of its latest acquisition. He was sitting at the desk in his new Zandax office in Ellis Habitat when his comm buzzed.

"Spencer here."

He listened for a moment, then stiffened and sat up ramrod straight.

"Yes, sir, of course, sir."

He set down his comm, then refreshed his display. In an instant, the scowling visage of his corporate up line replaced the logo on the screen.

"Spencer, we have a problem."

"Whatever it is, sir, I'll get on it."

The scowl relaxed for a moment, replaced by an attempted smile.

"Spencer, we've discovered that a former engineer at Zandax, Albert Salondo, has been poking his nose where it doesn't belong."

"Do we have him in custody, sir?"

"No, and he left before we got any information. We can't find him, and that's where you come in."

"If he's still on Ellis, sir, we'll find—"

"He's not. But we think one of his collaborators is."

"What information do we have on this collaborator, sir?"

"His name is Logan Rhodes. He's an independent investigator."

"What's our exposure here, sir?"

"We don't know yet. That's why we need to get him, ASAP. And then shut him down."

"If I take your meaning, sir, we are to—"

"Make sure he's never a problem for us again, Spencer. Ever."

The display went blank.

Spencer sat back in his chair and stared at the black screen.

"ROE-LAWN-DOE. WHAT KINDA candy-ass name is that, anyhow? Ask me, it sounds like something you'd name your poodle, right, Mahon?" Field Tech II Aram Terzakian flashed a toothy grin at the new trainee, Erik Mahon.

Field Tech I Rolando Sims sat, boots on the desktop, tapping icons on a tablet. He took a bite of a doughnut from the box supplied daily to the Zandax security office. Shifting his languid, hooded eyes toward Terzakian, he hoisted the proverbial middle finger.

"Yeah, well, nobody asked you, turd sack." Sims dropped his empty coffee cup onto the floor and watched the cleaner bot roll over and grind it up.

Terzakian was tall, well-muscled, and had black hair cut in military fashion. Despite his intimidating physique, his crooked grin and easy-going nature soon put most people at ease.

Sims and Terzakian made eye contact, then looked at Mahon. The trainee sat on the edge of his chair, his smooth face frozen in wary tension. He flashed a look of nervous uncertainty at the two older men.

Terzakian winked at him. "Relax, Mahon. We don't go on shift for an hour. Here," he pointed to the coffee and pastries, "grab some zuzus." Giving Mahon a conspiratorial nod, he slid his boots off the desktop, sat up, and fished a doughnut from the box. Mahon relaxed, but his serious expression remained.

Sims's chair creaked as he rocked it back onto its rear legs.

"You know, turd sack, the day they issued brains, you must have been in the head playing with your pecker."

Terzakian looked at him. "Why, Sims, I would never deprive you of that pleasure."

Sims rocked his chair forward and then shot to his feet.

"Well, gentlemen, I need to go shake the dew off my lily."

Terzakian stood and stretched.

"Yeah, time to tap a kidney before we go on shift. Hold down the fort, Mahon."

In the restroom, Sims glanced at Terzakian. "How do you think the kid's doing?"

"It's a tad soon to tell. He's a little nervous. He needs to get into the field. You know, Sims, we have to stop meeting like this. People might start to talk."

"Wow. That's original."

They washed their hands at the sink. While Terzakian dried his hands, Sims held his wet hands away from his uniform as they headed back to the briefing room. When they entered, just as Sims passed Mahon, he shook his wet hands, spraying the young trainee.

"Damn!" Sims barked. "I just hate it when I piss all over my hands."

Mahon recoiled in horror, then relaxed, giving Sims a wary look.

"I haven't seen that one in a while, sir."

9

"Mahon, you can skip the 'sir'. Here, we're all just field grunts." Sims's pocket comm vibrated, and he inspected the display. "Hot news flash, lads: staff meeting in the conference room in five minutes."

Terzakian rolled his eyes. "I can hardly wait."

TERZAKIAN, SIMS, AND Mahon took seats in the rear of the conference room. The buzz of low chatter, punctuated by snickers and creaking chairs, faded to silence when a stranger in a well-tailored business suit entered the room. He strode to the front and faced the gathering. Rapping a knuckle on the podium, he stood glaring at the audience.

"You're wondering what this is about. Well, listen and learn. My name is Spencer, Director Spencer. As of 0900 this morning, Zandax was acquired by the Marsh Corporation."

The room was silent. Spencer stared at the group. Terzakian, wearing a bland smile, rocked his chair back and put his hands behind his head. Spencer glared at him.

"You. In the back. Do you find this amusing?"

Terzakian folded his arms across his chest and rocked his chair forward.

"Where's Marty Liu?"

Spencer fixed him with a reptilian stare. "And you are …?"

"Aram Terzakian."

Spencer's eyebrows knitted as he leaned over the podium.

"Well, Aram Terzakian, the whereabouts of Martin Liu are not your concern. From now on, you will report to Mr. Vierek, your new supervisor."

Sims nudged Terzakian. "Picture your fist, impacting that face at high velocity."

Terzakian gazed at Spencer.

"So, Director Spencer, are you here to give us a pep talk or just wave your dick in our faces?"

The room erupted in gasps, snickers, and outright laughter.

Sims elbowed him and grinned. "Is that how you welcome our brand-new director?"

Spencer's face blanched, then went fire-engine red as he leaned forward over the podium.

"Now you listen to me, mister," he said through gritted teeth. "I don't know how my predecessor handled things here, and I don't care. I won't tolerate insubordination or disrespect. Do I make myself clear?" He looked at the group. "Dismissed!"

FLOYD STILLMAN HAD a rangy build, a lean, chiseled face, and a confident, good-humored nature. He stood in the Hawkington transport terminal and adjusted his rucksack. Under a dim yellow light, three people queued up before a podium. Behind it, a flight attendant scrolled through lists on a display. Floyd took his place in the queue behind a stocky young man holding a duffel bag and a rucksack. Next was a slight, lively young woman with tan skin and black hair tied into an intricate knot on the back of her head. She turned her luminous brown eyes back at Floyd and smiled. At the front of the line stood a graying middle-aged man of average height and build in a worn blue jumpsuit. The attendant scanned his ID and then examined the next item on the display.

Floyd leaned close to the young man ahead of him.

"I guess we're headed to the same place. I'm Floyd Stillman."

They shook hands.

"Julio Ortiz. 2060RT2 is what I was told. Are you a miner?"

"Yup."

"Ditto." Julio pointed to the young woman ahead of him. "She's Bhani."

She turned and extended her hand.

"Bhanupriya Oka. Welcome to the crew, Floyd. The old sourpuss up front is Roy Frankhauser."

"I heard that, Oka." Roy looked back at the crew and winked.

She cupped her hands and spoke in Roy's direction.

"Roy's alright, when he takes the stick out of his ass."

Roy looked at the ceiling and shook his head.

Floyd laughed. "I gather Roy's the supervisor?"

Julio caught Floyd's eye. "More like 'stupid-visor', but if you tell him I said that, I'll deny it."

"Keep digging, Ortiz."

Floyd grinned at Julio. "It looks like I've got some catching up to do here."

THE FLIGHT ATTENDANT tapped console icons, and the boarding hatch opened. She gave Roy a nod, and he looked back at the crew. "OK. It looks like we're ready to go."

They entered the shuttle and strapped into their seats.

Bhani looked at Floyd. "Floyd, tell us about yourself."

"Well, I'm from Swopes Holler, a small town in West Virginia. Born and raised there. After high school, community college in mechatronics, and then some mining tech work, I went to West

Virginia U for civil and mining engineering. Then, I got an internship with Alpha Zubrin. After finishing my degree, AZ transferred me here."

Julio stared at Floyd, his eyes fixed in reptilian wariness.

"So, tell me, Floyd, is it true that West Virginia is full of inbred pig fuckers?"

Bhani's face went wide with mock outrage. "Julio!" she jabbed him with her elbow.

Floyd grinned at Julio. "Absolutely. And when we run low on inbred pigs, we just order a fresh batch from California."

Julio gave Floyd an appraising look. "Welcome to the crew, Floyd."

Bhani slid over into the vacant seat next to Roy and studied him.

"Something on your mind, Bhani?"

"Yes, Roy. I'm curious about what it will be like at the mine site."

"Well, you'll be finding out."

"I've never been anywhere like that. Do you have any pointers or advice for me?"

Roy thought for a moment. "It's best to not have any expectations."

"Easier said than done."

"What are you expecting?"

"It's hard to pin down. I expect it will be scary and interesting."

"Are you worried?"

She shrugged. "Not really, but I know it could get hairy if something goes wrong."

Roy looked at Bhani for a moment. "There are risks. The mine is remote, so there's a lag between calling for help and getting it.

The emergency shelters will keep you alive for a while, if you get to one in time. An Earth-side analogy is living in a module on the ocean floor at its deepest point. If you lose power, if there is a hull breach, or if the atmosphere control fails, you die, maybe quickly, maybe not; timely rescue is unlikely. You're at the mercy of the technology and your team members.

"The accommodations are spartan, and the novelty of near-weightlessness is short-lived. It raises hell with your body, and you'll dream about Serenity's gym. It's essential to get along well with the crew. Small personality ticks can boil up into ugly situations if people aren't careful and disciplined."

Bhani flashed him a nervous grin. "Roy, I hope this is not your idea of a pep talk."

"You're trained for this, Bhani. Just focus on doing your job and looking after the others."

2

LOGAN SPRINTED THROUGH the alley behind Zandax. He headed into a boneyard strewn with broken machinery, piles of empty crates, and stacked building materials. Ducking behind a crate, he crouched and listened while catching his breath. Moving between rows of stacked containers, he raced to the end of the yard, then through a series of alleys behind rows of blocky buildings. He took cover at the edge of a large courtyard. With shaking fingers, he pulled out his map of Ellis Habitat.

I have to get out of sight.

SIMS WALKED INTO the squad room and waved his pocket comm.

"We have to go catch someone who just left the building, supposedly armed and dangerous."

Terzakian's eyes widened. "What? Who?"

Sims shook his head.

"Some mutt in a brown suit. And Spencer wants him 'dead or alive'. His exact words."

"He couldn't have meant that literally."

"Did he strike you as someone who kids around?"

Terzakian shook his head. "That can't be right. What does Vierek say?"

"Vierek is out of the loop."

"Spencer doesn't have that kind of authority."

"Tell that to the Marsh suits. They own the place now."

"Maybe. But they don't own us."

Terzakian looked at Mahon and Krug, another trainee. "Alright lads, we have some actual work to do. The boneyard, pronto. Krug, laser carbine, and stick with Sims. Mahon, twelve bore, and you're with me. No shooting unless I give the word. Understood?" Both men nodded. Terzakian picked up a silenced ballistic sniper rifle, and they jogged to the stairs.

IN THE ALLEY, Terzakian and Mahon moved between points of concealment, where they paused and scanned the area. Terzakian turned to Mahon.

"Follow the right perimeter. We'll get info from the drone." He pointed up at a small dot flying fifty meters overhead. "No shooting without my orders."

"Sir, Director Spencer ordered me to shoot the suspect."

Terzakian stared at him. "Shoot?"

"His exact word, sir."

"Mahon, I'm countermanding that order as of now, understood?"

Wide-eyed, Mahon nodded. "Understood, sir."

"Mahon, make a report of everything Spencer said to you. Include dates, times, and places. Attach copies of any messages he sent. That's so none of this blows back on you or Krug. Give copies to me and Sims, but nobody else."

A wave of relief swept over the young trooper's face. "Yes, sir."

Terzakian slapped him on the shoulder. "OK. Let's go. Get in position."

"Yes, sir."

Mahon took off in a crouching trot, and Terzakian watched him disappear into the boneyard.

Terzakian's comm hummed, and Mahon's voice came on. He had spotted the target. The tiny map on Terzakian's comm showed a flashing red dot about a hundred meters ahead and to the left, behind a stack of boxes. He moved forward, his rifle at the ready, and soon had the target in his telescopic sight. The man was of medium build, wore a brown suit, and shouldered a small pack as he crouched behind an equipment crate. He was clearly frightened, his eyes darting around. Terzakian's trigger finger extended along his rifle's receiver as he moved his scope over the target. The man appeared to be unarmed. Terzakian lowered his rifle and tapped his comm.

"Mahon, see if you can catch him, but don't hurt him." Terzakian watched through his rifle scope as Logan disappeared into the maze of crates and equipment.

After a while, Terzakian's comm hummed again.

"Sir, I lost him. Should I keep looking?"

"No, Mahon. The guy's not a threat, and he won't get off the habitat. We'll find him if we have to." He switched comm channels. "Sims, we're done. All rally on me. Time to head back."

IN THE ASTEROID 2060RT2 mine complex, Bhani, Floyd, and Julio finished their evening meal and drifted into the rec room.

Flopping onto a lounger, Floyd took his tablet from the side table and worked the screen.

"Oh yeah. Love it. Bhani, check this out." He held up the tablet.

Bubba's Big Book of Payback:

The Art and Science of Practical Retribution

by

Ray Bob Walker

Bhani had just taken a chair at the chess table. She looked at the tablet.

"Oh, give me a break, Floyd."

"I shit you not. And check out the author."

She inspected the tablet image.

"It figures. Look, when I said try reading a book, I didn't mean that."

Floyd settled back with his eyes half closed.

"Well, I forgot my copy of *The Exegesis of Philip K. Dick*. You best watch out now, Bhani. I'm liable to use some of this on you." He turned back to the tablet.

Julio, having watched the exchange, caught Bhani's eye. He pointed to the chessboard and raised his eyebrows. She inspected him.

"I'm not in the habit of entertaining troglodytes, but perhaps tonight I'll make an exception."

Fixing her with an evil leer, he settled into the opposite chair, rubbing his palms together.

"Oye, mamacita, troggie gonna crush you like a cucaracha."

She opened a beer and eyed him. "You laugh now, monkey boy, pay later."

And so they continued on, hunched over the chessboard, the

occasional gloating chuckle floating up, followed by an outraged growl. Glancing at the wall clock, Julio stood and stretched.

"We'll finish this ass kicking tomorrow. I'm hitting the sack."

She shrugged. "Fine. You're losing anyhow."

"Oh, yeah? We'll see about that tomorrow. Unless you bribe Floyd to rearrange the board."

She glared at Julio. He flashed her a smug grin, then turned and sauntered out the door.

Bhani moved to a chair near Floyd.

"So, Floyd, what's your family like? Assuming you have one."

He set down his tablet. "Bhani, don't assume anything around here."

"No, come on, seriously."

"Seriously? I'm not familiar with that word. But yeah, I have a family. Parents are still working, brothers, sisters, wife, all still living in Swopes Holler. What about you?"

"I grew up in New Delhi. Went to public school there, worked odd jobs, then got into IIT Kharagpur on a scholarship. Got degrees in chemical and mining engineering and wound up at Alpha Zubrin."

"What about your family?"

"My parents run a manufacturing business in New Delhi with my two brothers and a sister."

"How do they feel about you being here?"

"Probably the same way your family does."

"They weren't too thrilled about it. Neither was my wife when I told her. Lulu just gave me a look. Pretty clear what it meant, though."

A HUNDRED METERS from the Zandax facility, Logan kept his back against a wall, inched to the corner of the building, then peeked around the edge. Across the courtyard, a dozen civilians of varying age and gender shuffled into a rough queue in front of an officer holding a tablet. On either side of him were two grunts, swinging carbines about as they scanned the area. Logan watched the officer check each person's ID and, after a brief exchange, wave them on. He froze when a grunt looked in his direction, spat into a planter, checked his carbine's magazine, then returned his gaze to the queue. Logan exhaled and watched the officer study the credentials of a man dressed like Logan. He pulled back behind the blocky structure and saw a gray utility access node behind a bush several meters away.

The node was a composite cube three meters on a side. It was little more than a ventilation duct with a screened access port. Logan stepped behind the node and saw two young boys sitting in the greenery. They wore the same brown shirts and trousers and appeared less than ten years old. The boys looked up at Logan with pale, gaunt faces and terrified eyes.

Shit.

"Please don't hurt us, mister," said the larger one. "We weren't doing anything."

Logan squatted beside them and forced a smile.

"Hey, hey, it's alright, guys. I'm just a tourist like you. What're your names?"

The larger boy looked nervously about and flicked a twig from his hair.

"I'm Adrian, and he's Sebastian." He pointed to the smaller boy. "We were looking for bugs and got lost."

Logan eyed the access port. The screen was partly open, and two screws lay in the dirt.

"You might be onto something here, guys. Let's look for bugs in there."

He winked at them, and their taut, drawn faces relaxed into tentative smiles as Adrian attacked the remaining screws with a multi-tool. Sebastian, who looked younger, glanced around while Adrian worked. When the last screw fell free, they crawled through the opening, and Logan pulled the screen back into place.

A small overhead lamp threw faint yellow light over the node's interior. Cable bundles snaked from the end of a conduit through a meter-square floor opening, but there was space to slip past them. Logan pulled a pair of gloves from his pack.

"Alright, you wait here until I pull on this wire." He tugged a yellow cable strand, and the boys nodded in unison. Logan gripped the edge of the opening and then eased himself feet first into the dark.

When Logan's feet touched the floor, he crouched as his eyes adjusted to the gloom. A few meters away, a worker stooped over a cable bundle. The worker wore a bulky facial apparatus. With his peripheral vision blocked, he bobbed and shuffled along in the semi-darkness. A meter beyond the worker, dirty gray light filtered through an open door.

Logan gave the yellow strand a pull, then helped the boys down. He put a finger to his lips and pointed to the worker tending the cable bundles. The boys nodded, and they crept through the door to a stairwell. At the bottom, Logan worked a door latch, and they stepped outside into daylight. Beyond the alley lay a wooded draw.

Larger habitats in the Sol System had taken fleets of robots a decade or more to complete. Some included impressive natural landscaping. The draw snaked away from the building complex and into a forest. Logan could hear only the occasional chirping of birds ruffling in the foliage overhead as the trio moved in the shadows.

They walked in silence until Logan saw the dark outlines of a building behind a wall of leafy green. Light glinted from three transparent domes, each a dozen meters high. Composite tubular corridors three or four meters in diameter connected the domes to a central building. Logan's map showed no structures in the area. He motioned the boys to follow him into the brush by the nearest dome.

"I'll see what this is. You hide here until I come back." They nodded, and Logan crept over to an entrance. Inside, stairs led up to a well-lit atrium.

ON ITS MAIN floor were rows of hydroponic stations connected to a network of gurgling pipes and graced by a variety of green plants. Several rows down, a figure in a hooded work suit leaned over a tank, swaying to music playing from speakers mounted near the ceiling. Logan ran his fingers through his hair, then took a deep breath. He walked toward the figure, who turned and stood facing him.

She wore an ocular attachment over her left eye. A filigree of fine lines and curves detailed the large, emerald-green iris of her right eye. A spray of violet and gold freckles crossing her cheeks shifted as her pale-blue face relaxed. Her full, violet lips moved into a wary smile as she wiped her hands with a cloth hanging from her workbench. A device on her belt beeped, and she pressed a button to silence it. Shifting the ocular attachment away from her left eye, her gaze transformed into something like a frown.

"You aren't supposed to be here. How did you find my lab? And who are you?"

Logan, staring at the tiny gold triangles encircling her green irises, blinked, then shook his head. "I'm sorry. I must have gotten the wrong directions. My name is Logan Rhodes. What is this place?"

She stepped closer, studied him for a moment, then glanced at a data terminal. Her long blue fingers laced together at her waist.

"My security cam picked you up outside. What are you doing here?"

"I was out taking a walk with my sons and we got lost. They're waiting outside. I just need some directions, and we'll be on our way."

She shifted her lush violet lips to one side, shook her head, then turned toward a data terminal.

"In a minute. I need to check my culture." She worked her holographic console.

Logan looked over her shoulder at a display showing scrolling images of text and symbols.

"Did your security cams pick up anyone else?"

She tapped her console and inspected the display.

"No. Why?"

"I thought someone might be following us."

"Who?"

"I don't know; it was just a feeling."

Water splashed in a tank, and a cat-sized creature with a scaly, beaked head clutched the tank's edge with tiny black talons. It squawked and swished its tail back and forth in the water.

Logan stared at it as he lowered himself into a chair. "What is that?"

She grinned at him with perfect white teeth, her emerald eyes squinting with delight as the band of violet and gold freckles played over her nose and cheeks.

"That's a Yates hen. Isn't she cute?"

The creature gazed at Logan with large, black eyes and chirped.

"Oh yeah. Absolutely adorable. And a Yates hen is …?"

"Bio-engineered to live in the tanks. Alpha Zubrin scientists recently developed them. They lay edible eggs."

She snaked a finger into her jacket pocket, pulled out a yellow lump, and dropped it into the creature's open beak. It swallowed the morsel, squawked, then dove back into the hydroponic murk. She tapped a few icons and then frowned at the display.

"Uh-oh."

"What?" Logan sat up in his chair.

"These readings. Something's not …"

She drew a small pistol from the tool bag on her belt and pointed it toward the entrance. A loud crack and a bright flash erupted from the weapon's muzzle. Logan looked toward the door and saw Adrian lying on the floor, blood pulsing from a centimeter-size hole in his forehead. His body twitched, then was still. Logan, frozen in shock, gaped in disbelief.

"What the hell have you just done?"

"I'm going to count to three! If you don't come out with your hands up, I will kill you! One, two …"

Sebastian emerged from behind the tank, his hands in the air. The woman's face was now dark blue, the green of her irises replaced by a bottomless black.

"Get on the floor, face down, hands straight out from your sides. If you move, I will kill you." Sebastian did as he was told.

She swung her weapon at Logan, and with her free hand ran commands on the terminal. She scanned the display between glances at Sebastian and Logan, her weapon's aim shifting between them.

"It seems your sons were trying to run my data, plus a few other naughty little tricks. I want some answers. Now."

Logan held his shaking hands out, palms up, his eyes wide.

"They're not my sons. I don't know who they are. I found them on the way from Zandax Plaza. They seemed lost. I was going to drop them off somewhere they could get help. How could they run your data? They weren't even near a terminal."

"You chanced upon two innocent little boys along the way." She shook her head. "Pardon my skepticism, but you've brought two skin jobs into my lab. You've got some explaining to do."

"They looked like lost kids. I didn't know what they were. I went to Zandax for a business meeting. I wasn't expecting Marsh Corporation to be there. The plaza was crawling with Marsh thugs. I hoped I could get help here. My mistake."

Her skin color began fading back to light blue, the green returning to her eyes.

"Avala. My name is Avala. And you can put your hands down."

She turned and shot Sebastian in the head.

LOGAN STOOD LOOKING down at the two small, lifeless bodies lying in spreading crimson pools and stared at Avala.

"Who the hell are you?"

"I just told you."

"What's going on here? What is this place?"

"Not so fast, Logan."

She pulled a tablet from her tool bag, worked its touchscreen, and a robotic loader dumped the bodies into a port on the far wall. She tapped the screen again, and a smaller robot wheeled over and hosed the blood into a floor drain. Frowning, her right hip cocked, the toe of her left shoe tapping on the concrete floor, Avala folded her slender arms across her breasts. Her bottle-green eyes narrowed with a hint of amusement. "So, Logan, that's what you've brought me."

She walked to a terminal and inspected more scrolling displays.

"Their signals didn't get past my shielding, so we have a little time before Marsh starts a search. Tell me about yourself, Logan. Start with who you work for."

"I'm an independent consultant and investigator. Right now, I'm working, or was working, with an engineer at Zandax Corporation. Now that's out the window."

"I gather you didn't pick up on Marsh's plans for Zandax. In case you've been out of the sector for the last ten years, Marsh provides armed muscle for aggregations of power and money. Some were legal under the old regime. They still do as they please, keeping corporate names to appear as legitimate, civilized businesses."

"You can skip the patronizing lecture. I'm well aware of what Marsh is. I didn't know about its takeover of Zandax until I got there and learned that Marsh had fired my contact. The Marsh people wanted to interview me, but I was having none of it. And here I am."

"And here you are. Well alrighty then. I see you're in a bit of a pickle, and you need my help, so it would behoove you to tell me what you're really about and why you're in my lab."

"OK, I get it; you don't believe me. I guess I wouldn't either, but what I said was the truth. I went to Albert Salondo's Zandax office, and he wasn't there. Instead, there was some guy named Vierek. While I was there, I checked my comm and saw a message from Albert. He said Marsh had taken over Zandax, and I shouldn't go there. A bit late for that advice. Vierek said Al had been fired, and I was legally obligated to submit to an interrogation. I got a bad feeling, excused myself, and left by a back exit.

"I was being chased. I got the hell out of there. There were armed grunts on the plaza. Call me a wimp, but I have an aversion to weapons, especially when they might be used on me. I don't know anyone in Ellis Hab, so I wandered through the woods and stumbled onto this place; it didn't show up on my map. I know that sounds hinky, but it's the truth."

She worked her terminal and looked at the display.

"OK. You just passed the first test."

"What are you talking about?"

"Your biometric scan. I have sensors scattered about here that pick up all sorts of biological data about visitors to my lab. My data indicate a 96% probability you're not lying to me. So, I won't shoot you. Unless you seriously piss me off." Her lips curved into a smirk.

He inspected her face. "You're enjoying this."

Avala gave Logan an appraising look.

"Let's try this. I know you need help, and I suspect you might be able to help me. I don't limit my research to hydroponics. There, I've told you a bit more. Your turn."

"I'm a consultant and an investigator. Officially, I came to Ellis Hab to talk with Albert Salondo, a systems engineer. We were planning a project to help Ellis develop its infrastructure and manufacturing. My end was IT services planning, data collection and analysis, and financial planning; mostly basic stuff. Marsh blindsided me this morning. I forgot to turn on my comm when I got off the shuttle, so I didn't get Al's warning in time. You know the rest."

"Officially. What about unofficially?"

He nodded. "I'll get to that."

"Now is a good time, Logan."

"Unofficially, I was helping Al gather data on Marsh, in particular, details of its illegal activities in the sector. We intended to give the data to the sector attorney general when it was complete. Apparently, Marsh discovered what we were doing, and now they're after me, too. I'm worried about what they might do to Al; he's an old friend."

She went to her terminal, pecked a few icons, then studied the display.

"Marsh probably wanted to make sure you didn't take information or proprietary items. It regarded Zandax as a rival and a threat, hence the takeover. It doesn't like competition. And what's left of corporate regulations out here is unenforceable." She worked the console, inspected the display, then looked at him. "As of Marsh's arrival, Zandax Corporation is no longer in business. You can forget about that pay deposit."

He frowned, then leaned back in his chair, studying her.

"I have to assume they're after me for what Al and I were doing. So, where to from here?"

She sat up and pulled back her work suit hood, revealing a dense wave of braided sapphire-colored hair.

"I do more than biotech research. I'm also in the information business, which brings me to my next question. Are you interested in doing a little contract work for me?"

Swiveling his chair in random directions, Logan scratched his head and squinted at Avala.

"I'll probably regret it, but alright."

She inspected him with a level, neutral gaze, her blue face impassive.

"First, we have to arrange for you to disappear."

"So what I've done so far doesn't count?"

"No." She rotated her chair toward the console. "I mean formally disappear."

"I'm listening." He looked at her display. "What are you doing now?"

"I'm using an obsolete encryption algorithm to send a bogus message to a bogus consulting business, like the one you claim to run. OK. You have just departed Ellis Habitat and are en route to an undisclosed location. Marsh's new comm super is unqualified and is likely to buy it. We'll have a few days before someone competent shows up and figures it out. Marsh could be a problem for me."

"For us." He shot her a quizzical look tinged with annoyance. "And it's New World Consulting."

"What?"

"My business. It's called New World Consulting, and it's not bogus. But back to my 'disappearance'. What happens to me, to us, when Marsh figures out it's been had?"

"Oh gosh, I don't know," she said in an affected, giggly voice. "I guess we'll just have to improvise, won't we?" She gazed at him with amusement.

He gave her a narrow look. "Are you always like this?"

"Like what?" She inspected him with a slight smile on her violet lips.

"Your appearance, your behavior … you must know how they affect people."

She shrugged. "I don't get out much. Enlighten me."

"For starters, your skin, hair, eyes. I've seen some exotic personal mods, but nothing quite like what you have. Can you give me some background here?"

"Maybe later. Speaking of looks, right now you look like you could use a shower and clean clothes. There are empty apartments up on the second floor. Take your pick. They all have interesting views and some clean work suits. I'll see you here later, and we can fix something to eat."

Logan walked between the hydroponic station rows and up the stairs to the first apartment. It contained a kitchen, a living room, a bathroom, and two bedrooms, all furnished and clean. A sliding glass door opened onto a terrace with a view of dense green forest. In the distance, dark clouds obscured the habitat's far wall. He dropped his bag, closed his eyes, and took a deep breath of air just freshened by a cleansing rain.

In the bathroom, Logan took off his soiled, sweat-damp clothes, then showered, shaved, and brushed his teeth. Finding several clean work suits in a bedroom closet, he dressed and sat on the edge of the bed. He looked around, fell back, and closed his eyes.

3

THE EXPLOSION SMACKED Julio against the inside of the truck, stunning him. Ryan, the driver, was yelling, but Julio couldn't hear anything. Then a red spray and bloody fragments of glass splattered his face as bullets came through the windshield. Julio shook his head, wiped his eyes, and saw Ryan slumped motionless against the steering wheel. The truck slowed, stalled, and shuddered to a halt.

Julio awoke in his bunk, his underwear and sheets damp with sweat. In the dim yellow light, he saw Floyd and Bhani looking at him, concern on their faces.

"Julio," Floyd said, "you were having a nightmare."

He sat up and rubbed his face.

"Yeah, sorry, I ..." Bhani handed him a glass of water, and he drank it in three gulps. "Thanks. I'll be OK." He stood and pulled the sheets off his bunk. They watched him, exchanging worried looks. "It's alright. I'm good now."

Floyd and Bhani went back to their cubicles.

Julio showered, put on clean underwear, and lay on his bunk. The faint glow of a corridor lamp was the only visible indicator of his location.

Julio opened his eyes. The red LED digits of the nightstand clock showed 02:13. He sat up, swung his legs over the bunk's edge, and stood in the semi-darkness. The smooth composite deck was cool under his feet. Wearing cotton overalls, he wandered out to the rec room, filled a glass with water from the sink, then sat on a lounger. He sipped the water and gazed at the wall. The only sounds were the faint humming and clicking of mine machinery. He finished the water, then went back to his bunk.

THE MINE COMPLEX'S breach alarm went off, and Roy Frankhauser awoke with a start. The honking was loud enough to rouse anyone with a pulse. He switched on his nightstand lamp, then jumped over to the control terminal and sat at the console. Flashing display icons showed backup power was online, and all local hatch backup power supplies were functioning. He looked out the window, and his eyes widened.

Floyd was writing a letter to Lulu when the rec room lights went out. An instant later, the yellow emergency lamps came on, and the alarm went off. He took his tablet and bolted from the room.

Julio flashed awake and sat up in his bunk. "What the hell?"

"Atmosphere loss alarm," Bhani called from the next cubicle. "A meteorite strike. We're on backup power."

Emergency corridor lights pulsed through the dorm hatch window. Julio jumped out of his bunk and put on his S3, the standard pressure suit for outside work. Bhani grabbed her buzzing personal comm off the nightstand.

"Listen up," Roy announced, his voice tinny over the small

speaker. "We have a situation. There's a breach in the exterior tube and some local depressurization. Put on your S3s and stay put. If you don't have an S3, go to the nearest shelter. We're on backup power, so try to conserve it. This is not a drill, people. Roy out."

Roy stared out the window, then went to the control console. He put on a headset and switched to a network link.

"This is Roy Frankhauser on 2060RT2. Connect me to Ved Rao. Yes, I know it's the middle of the night. Get him."

The dorm unit now functioned on limited power. In the glow of an emergency light, Bhani put on her S3.

Julio appeared in the doorway.

"Where's Floyd? He's not in the sleeping area."

She shook her head.

"Then either the washroom or rec room. Or a shelter, number two or three."

Her suit comm clicked, and Roy's voice came on.

"Bhani, is everyone in the crew quarters?"

"Roy, I'm in the dorm with Julio, and we're suited up. Floyd must have gone to a shelter. What's going on?"

"Just sit tight. I'll get back to you."

A light flashed on the display, and Roy switched channels.

"Ved, Roy Frankhauser here. Yes, I know what time it is. We have a situation. Do you remember what I said about that external corridor? Guess what just happened? Five minutes ago. The crew? Two are OK. One is missing. Ved, you need to look at it. What exactly? A breach. A type-two breach. What's a type-two breach? You'll see when you get here. And bring Lauren Chen. Yes, I'm serious."

FLOYD SPRINTED TO the shelter twenty meters down the corridor. Emergency drills had honed his reflexes, and his movements were automatic. The shelter door slid open as he approached and then automatically closed behind him. He punched two buttons on the door console, and the door slid back open. He pulled an S3 from a locker, set the helmet and gloves on the floor, and began putting on the torso unit. The suit's comm was missing. The shelter's wall comm allowed only communication with someone nearby in the corridor. Floyd glanced back out the open shelter door. The main corridor lights were off, replaced by the sickly yellow of an emergency lamp.

He faced out into the corridor. "Stillman here! I'm in shelter number three. I'll keep the hatch open as long as I can, so if anyone's coming, they need to get here ASAP."

A calm, disinterested female voice came over the speaker on the shelter's interior wall.

"A class one emergency has been detected. The shelter will lock down in exactly one minute. Counting down now. Sixty, fifty-nine, fifty-eight ..."

Floyd scowled at the speaker.

"Hey out there! The shelter's locking down!"

Just under a minute later, the door slid shut and locked with a clank.

A small amber light shone from the shelter ceiling. A wall-mounted display showed a normal atmosphere out in the corridor. Floyd punched the door switch, to no effect. The door's release code was not posted nearby. He grabbed the flashlight hanging by the door and began searching the shelter's cabinets.

"OK. Water, rations, medical kit, comm ..."

He played the flashlight beam over the comm's keypad. He followed the instructions on a small laminated card and punched in the connection to the front office.

"Hey, this is Stillman. I'm in shelter number three. What's going on?"

There was no reply, just a faint, steady hiss. The radio's battery level showed less than five percent. Floyd shook his head, then tossed the radio onto a shelf. He took a deep breath and continued inspecting the locker's contents.

JULIO AND BHANI'S suit comms clicked, and Roy's voice came on.

"Any developments there?"

"No. Roy, what's going on?"

"You'll get details later, Julio. Sit tight."

Julio flipped his suit comm off, then moved closer to Bhani, their helmets touching.

"We need to find Floyd. I'm going to look around."

She nodded. "He must be in a shelter."

Julio opened the hatch and stepped into the corridor. The hatch, working on backup power, slid shut behind him. Bhani went to her cubicle and sat on the bunk. Her S3 utility module hummed, and she felt the reassuring warmth of the suit's heating system. She toggled her comm switch. "Roy, give me a status update ASAP."

IN THE DIM light of the corridor, wall sensors showed normal atmosphere composition, pressure, and temperature. Julio moved his flashlight beam over the rec room hatch. Its status display also showed normal conditions in the room. He went to the airlock leading to the exterior corridor and the office. The display by the first airlock hatch showed that normal functioning was available via backup power. Julio opened the hatch and stepped into the vestibule. The hatch closed behind him. He moved forward to face the next hatch, which led to the decontamination and transfer chamber. He opened it, stepped through, and it closed behind him.

The airlock's status panel lights showed the air evacuation mechanism sucking the air out of the transfer chamber. The system then filtered, disinfected, and stored it for later recharging. A flashing green light showed it was safe to proceed. He opened the exterior hatch and stepped into the dark, depressurized corridor. To his left, he saw the breach.

Julio stared at it for a few minutes, then pulled a cam from his S3's pocket. He flipped its power switch, then spoke into his suit comm.

"Roy, look." He passed the cam's optical sensor over the breach in a slow sweeping motion.

"Yeah, Julio, I saw it through my suite window."

There was a smooth, elliptical hole in the tube large enough to walk through. The composite corridor supported several utility links, but only the power line was cut.

"I'm going to see what the hull's exterior looks like."

Julio stepped through the breach and onto the asteroid's surface. To his left lay an ink-dark range of low, jagged hills and rock formations, impenetrable and barren. He looked to his right and saw an elliptical section of the hull leaning next to the breach hole—it had been removed with surgical precision. Julio's right hand reached to his hip for the holstered weapon that wasn't there.

Julio continued around the office to the front hatch opposite the breach. He saw nothing unusual until he aimed his flashlight beam at the hatch lock. He leaned close and saw two thin scratches no wider than a hair on the button opening the hatch. A bead of sweat trickled down his right armpit as he recorded an image of the hatch lock control. Julio pocketed his cam and went through the hatch.

He worked his way through the crew unit corridor, checking inside the rec room, the bathroom, the kitchen, the dining area, and the control room. He came to shelter number three and checked the atmosphere wall display. The air numbers were normal. Julio removed his S3 helmet, tapped on the shelter door, then worked its exterior comm interface.

"Floyd, are you in there?"

"Julio! I can't find the door code."

"I don't have it. Hang on for a second."

Julio tapped Roy's extension on his comm.

"Roy, Floyd's in shelter number three. Atmosphere's good in this corridor. We need the shelter's door code."

A FEW MINUTES later, the shelter door slid open and Floyd stepped out.

"What's going on?"

"Something strange, Floyd. I'm going into the mine." Julio put his S3 helmet back on, and Floyd headed for the dorm unit.

Julio worked his way into the mine. He inspected the stacks of boxes, rows of gray lockers, and ore containers. The tractors and service robots were all motionless. He headed down the recently bored tunnel. The drilling had exposed many gas vents of various sizes, some over a meter in diameter. Recording images with his cam, he walked near the side of a trail of unfamiliar markings in the floor dust, taking care not to disturb them. His steps raised clouds of the dust that floated up into a hazy, translucent wake behind him. At each junction in the tunnel, he marked location numbers on the wall and made a sketch of his route on his tablet.

At the tunnel's end, the idle boring machine awaited maintenance. The tunnel wall had a ragged opening about a meter and a half high. Julio crouched and shuffled through it into darkness. He stood and swept his flashlight's beam around the interior of a vent chamber. It contained a structure covering an area of twenty square meters. It was about three meters high with a curved, fluted wall. The wall was flat black, its surface smooth, with a detectable texture. He moved to the edge of the chamber, climbed onto a rock, and looked at the structure's top. There were two dark hexagonal openings, and what looked like four more, capped with smooth, black hexagonal plates.

MAGDI EL-SAID, VICE-PRESIDENT of Operations at Hawkington, was a man of exquisite taste. That was clear, from his expensive tailored suits to the impressive art work that adorned his spacious and opulently furnished office. With a lithe, athletic build, developed from years of competitive saber dueling, to a handsome face and a warm, ingratiating manner, he had gained a reputation for excellence among the Alpha Zubrin administrative staff. His engineering accomplishments dispelled rumors he had wangled his position through mere political maneuvering. Trappings of success and power notwithstanding, Magdi was foremost a creature of the scientific method. This formed the basis of his perceptual apparatus, a trait he shared with Dr. Ved Rao, head of the research and development division and Magdi's best friend.

He was scrolling through mineral extraction and processing plans when his desk comm buzzed. The receptionist's voice came through as a tinny, blaring monotone.

"Dr. El-Said, Dr. Chen is here. And a Mr. Zubie."

Magdi closed his eyes, took a deep breath, and exhaled. He pushed back from the desk and rubbed his face.

"OK, Jan, send them in." He ran a hand through his hair and buttoned his jacket.

Lauren Chen, dressed in a plain business suit, strode into Magdi's office. In her arms she clutched a large, shaggy gray cat, who gazed placidly at Magdi. He stood, shot his cuffs, and walked around the desk.

"Lauren, it's good to see you."

She flashed him a strained smile. "Magdi, why are we here at seven in the morning?"

He leaned against the desk and folded his arms.

"Just keeping you on your toes, Lauren. I don't want you getting lazy on me."

He turned his attention to the cat. It yawned, displaying an impressive array of long white teeth.

Lauren gazed at him, unblinking, the corners of her lips twitching.

"Hilarious. The 'but seriously' part better be good."

He regarded her with an appraising gaze. "Remember our last talk? Remember what I said?"

"This must be extra rich, Magdi, or you wouldn't be trying to change the subject so soon."

He stepped back behind the desk, sat, and reached for a small notepad. She leaned over and set the cat, Zubie, on the desk. The cat hopped over a stack of papers and into Magdi's lap, where it sat purring. He stroked the cat as it ran a raspy, wet tongue over his fingers. He scribbled a note on the pad, then turned it so Lauren could read it.

Room bugged

He pointed to the ceiling and gave her a tight smile. She nodded in understanding.

"So, what's the deal?"

"Mineral 207-D."

Magdi folded his arms and watched with amusement as a sardonic grin spread across Lauren's face.

"And ...?"

"And Ved wants you at a remote site to help fine-tune the processing."

She pursed her lips and looked at the ceiling.

"I expect you to make it worth my while. And here's part of the deal: if I go, Zubie goes too."

Magdi pushed his chair away from the desk and laced his fingers behind his head. Leaning back, he frowned and shifted his eyes up at the network of dome supports. Beyond the transparent ceiling loomed the dark Martian sky.

"Lauren, there are reasons we don't allow animals at remote sites."

Her eyes widened. She leaned over the desk and put her hands on the hard copy, her eyes boring into his. "Magdi, Zubie is not an animal. He's a kitty cat. Civilized people know the difference."

"My uncle has a great recipe for—"

"Don't start with me."

He leaned back in his chair and shook his head.

"If I make a policy exception for you, Lauren, I'll have to make one for everybody else. Ergo, no policy." He gave her a mock-serious frown. "Result: corporate collapse, chaos, mass starvation, and no more free gym membership."

She pressed her thighs against the desk and looked down at him. Her dark gaze intensified under arched eyebrows, her lips pursed. She braced her hands on the desk, then leaned down close and stared at him with large almond eyes, her nose three centimeters from his.

"You know, Magdi, I've always had a weak spot for your bullshit, but not this time." She stood and folded her arms. "Zubie goes. End of discussion."

"OK. Just give me one good reason for taking this silly cat."

"Mister Zubie! Did you hear what this oaf just called you?"

She looked back at Magdi and regarded him with frank satisfaction.

"Zubie's my research assistant."

Magdi closed his eyes.

"OK, but Zubie absolutely will not be drawing a salary." He opened his eyes. "And quit looking so smug. The board's already up my ass, so I need solid results from you and Ved."

"Magdi, have I ever let you down?"

He watched as the cat rolled onto its back and pawed his jacket buttons and tie.

"Do you really want to go there? Let's take a walk. There's some recent work in hydroponics I want you to see."

Magdi stood, set Zubie in his chair, then checked his jacket buttons. Lauren called to Zubie, and he hopped up and ran across the desktop, leaving a wake of scattered hard copy. Scooping him up, she strode out the door. Magdi swiped cat hair from his jacket as he admired the view of her departure.

He punched a button on his desk comm. "Jan, Dr. Chen and I will be in hydroponics if anyone needs me." He straightened his tie, then followed Lauren and Zubie out into the corridor.

She looked at him with narrowed eyes.

"Mineral 207-D? I can hardly wait for this one."

He closed his eyes and nodded.

"Ever since that name was cooked up as a prank, some people assume high intrigue when they hear it. Now it's an inside joke."

"We should ask people to stop using that expression."

"People need to have their fun, but at least one board member is taking it seriously, and he wants a sample."

"Tell him we're a long way from having the process dialed in, and he'll just have to wait. Unless the board's willing to pay for more expensive fuck-ups."

"As a matter of fact, Lauren, they are. And I don't think I can keep a straight face long enough to explain to him what Mineral 207-D means. Best to just let him dream and scheme."

Lauren frowned. "Maybe, but he's causing trouble. Should I talk to him?"

"No. He would think you're trying to intimidate him, and he would get worse."

Her eyes narrowed. "Are you talking about Bernie Grant?"

"The very same."

"What is with that guy?"

"Inherited wealth. He's never actually worked for a living, but he's an expert on everything, especially things he knows nothing about."

"I heard he got rich developing Grant Holdings."

Magdi shook his head.

"That's bullshit. His father developed and ran Grant Holdings. Bernie was just a front man until his father died. When Bernie turned eighteen, he got access to a huge trust fund set up by his grandfather and started working overtime at pissing it away. Later, Bernie tried to run Grant Holdings and made a mess of it. He got fat and mean after a string of bankruptcies and dwindling capital forced him to sell most of the business. Bernie still pretends he's a mogul. He'd be pathetic if he weren't so disgusting."

"I can tell you like him."

Midway down the deserted corridor, Lauren stopped, leaned against a rail, and gazed out a window.

Magdi stood next to her and looked around.

"Someone else on the board heard a rumor that the competition is working on the same ore type as one of our groups. We're looking into it. If it's true, we'll need to verify their source and process. If anyone presses you, just say you're at the site to investigate this—"

She closed her eyes.

"Mineral 207-D, at seven in the morning. I must have screwed up in a previous life."

"Something else going on at the site. You'll see when you get there."

Lauren frowned in concentration.

"I'm detecting the distinct sensation of smoke being blown up my ass. Why is that, Magdi?"

"Lauren, all I know is Ved wants you at the site. He assured me it's important, and he wants you there this morning."

She shot him an irritated look and folded her arms. "Then I want carte blanche."

He nodded. "You'll have it."

SITTING IN HIS new Zandax office, Vierek looked around, rested his hands on the desktop, and scooted the plush, swiveling chair back and forth. His starched corporate shirt collar pinched his neck, but Spencer had insisted that Vierek wear the suit. So, there he was, pretending to be one of the Zandax office pogues whom he had escorted off the premises several days before. He had been told to man Salondo's desk and handle anyone who appeared to be connected with Salondo or Logan Rhodes. They were to be searched and taken to an interrogation site.

Now Vierek was absorbing up line shit over the escape. A puke in a cheap brown suit had shown up, saying he had an appointment with Salondo. He left before security could to catch him. Spencer said he considered putting Vierek in charge of chasing down said puke, but he would probably fuck that up too. While he pondered his situation, the desk comm buzzed.

Vierek picked up the handset.

"Yes. Yes, sir. No, sir, I don't know where they are, sir. We can't get any signals from their chips. They're either in a shielded area or destroyed. The last location we have was the southeast corner of the main complex courtyard. No, sir, we have no reports. I know, sir. Terzakian's squad is looking for them. Yes, sir. Right away, sir."

Vierek swore under his breath, slammed the handset into its cradle, then closed his eyes and gritted his teeth. Grabbing the handset again, he punched a number on the interface.

"Sims? Vierek here. Listen, Spencer's got a major bug up his ass over those two little skin jobs we sent out a couple of days ago, Frick and Frack. What? OK, Sebastian and Adrian, whatever. Anyway, Sebastian and Adrian have gone missing, and Spencer's pissed. I told him you guys were out looking for them. Hey, would you stop yelling and just listen? Did you check the machine shop ventilation system? Yeah, the shielding is complete now. That would explain why we're not getting signals past there. Right. I need you to find those two little bionic pains in the ass. Yeah, I know, I owe you, fuck-you-very-much."

Vierek slammed the handset down and jerked the cap off an antacid bottle. He shook several tablets into his mouth, then sat back and glared at the desktop display.

4

THE EMERGENCY REPAIR module had landed that morning one hundred meters from the Asteroid 2060RT2 mine complex. Inside the module, the echoing clack of boot heels grew louder in the corridor leading to Jeff Mullen's cubicle. The casters on his chair rattled as he pushed away from the terminal. A thin, solitary figure in a gray work suit, topped by an unkempt shock of prematurely graying black hair, Jeff leaned back, closed his eyes, and rubbed his face. He looked out the hatch at the small, dim yellow lights arrayed along the corridor overhead. They vibrated in a barely perceptible, high-frequency flicker that gave Jeff a headache, one he knew he would have until he got off this bloody asteroid.

The heel clacking stopped, and Dr. Ved Rao's impassive brown face appeared in the hatchway. He nodded to Jeff, then gazed with satisfaction at the filigree of plumbing, wires, and displays interlaced on the module's curved wall. Anything technical interested Ved, and the more complex, the better. Ved was the senior R and D scientist at Alpha Zubrin's Hawkington branch. But he preferred a laboratory or remote site over an office suite or boardroom. He favored short-sleeved shirts and work clothes over a business suit, which he wore only when Magdi insisted. Ved ranked substance above image. Raised in a Hindu family, he had absorbed a deep reverence for living things. He claimed no religion for himself, but he acknowledged that cultures with strong spiritual systems withstood adversity. Magdi and Lauren were long-time friends of the Rao family and were frequent guests at their home. Ved's wife, Meeri, prepared traditional Indian meals while the precocious Rao children, Onir and Chandani, engaged Magdi and Lauren in long discussions and spirited debates.

JEFF TAPPED A stylus against the chair arm and looked at Ved.

"We've got a problem seating the grapples. The tech at Hawkington loaded the wrong drill bits."

Ved leaned against the wall and inspected Jeff. "So just use cables for now."

"It's not clear to me why we're here, Ved."

"We're here because Roy Frankhauser asked for us, because of the tube breach."

"For routine repair work?"

Ved folded his arms and looked at the ceiling.

"Obviously, Jeff, it's not routine. Are you paying attention?"

Jeff massaged his eyebrows, then waved his hands at the displays.

"You think I'm playing video games here?" He leaned back in his chair. "Tell Magdi if he doesn't give me a raise I'll fly over there and pee on that fancy rug he brought up from Cairo."

Ved grinned. "Just what we need, another malcontent—a rug-peeing malcontent, no less." His eyes flicked across the display bank, a sheen of moisture on his face. "What's the latest on the grapple?"

"Joe Leighton's on it. He should report in any minute."

Ved looked at a wall clock. "What's he doing now?"

Jeff inspected several displays and then operated a console.

"I'm bringing him up. Watch that monitor." He pointed at a display. "That's our hull cam. We'll see him in a minute. He took a chisel out to seat talon number six into the rock." Jeff put on a headset and adjusted the mic. "Joe, can you hear us?"

A metallic voice blared from the wall speaker.

"Yeah, Jeff. I'm at the talon. It's not gripping properly. I should have a temporary fix soon. We need those drill bits to do it right, but the module's not going to float away. Where's the breach? I can't see it from here."

Ved put on a headset and tapped the mic.

"On the other side of the tube. Roy has the mine crew working on it."

Jeff looked at Ved. "Why are we here if the mine crew is making the repair?"

"To collect data for a study Magdi wants done."

THE HARD COPY notice taped to the mine office's hatch announced a new occupant:

Dr. Lauren Chen
Science and Engineering Group
Alpha Zubrin Technologies Corporation

Lauren sat at a holoterminal, talking into her headset.

"Yes, I know. We're getting the data now. Well, you'll just have to wait. I'll get a sample to you as soon as we have one. Yes, I understand." She rolled her eyes at the ceiling and shook her head. Punching a console icon, she looked toward the hatch and saw Roy leaning against the frame.

He gave her a weary smile.

"Let me guess. The operation has just started, and they already want a sample."

"Yup. I told them it will get there when it gets there."

"A reminder of why I'm here and not back there."

"Which staff comedian came up with the name 'Mineral 207-D'?"

"No clue, too many possibilities."

Lauren leaned back and stretched. "And this mine is now 'Site 1287.'"

Roy nodded. "The name change adds a hint of secrecy. Snoops will assume we're here studying an ore code named Mineral 207-D."

"A red herring."

"That's the idea, but it's not clear who's being fooled."

"Right. 'Three can keep a secret if two are dead'. Was that Groucho Marx?"

"Benjamin Franklin, as I recall."

"Who would believe this?"

"No one paying attention," Roy said. "But greed, ego, and ambition are reliable distractions. A potentially lucrative ore process is more interesting than a mere hull breach, which wouldn't explain senior scientists being here."

"We'd better hope this works. I'm already imagining breathless news feeds all over Sol System."

He shrugged. "I wouldn't worry. If needed, it's easy to crank up a story about why the breach investigation is so important. Just use the word 'proprietary' a lot and say you can't go into details."

"Forgive me if I'm not so confident."

THE EMERGENCY REPAIR module used mechanical talons to attach to the slick, uneven rock surface. Joe Leighton was preparing a spot for a grapple. Movement required slow, deliberate steps over the asteroid's dusty surface. Shifting his grip on module handholds, he positioned a power chisel. Low-gravity movement required calculated precision. The surface texture varied from pocked to glassy-smooth. A slippery layer of powdery dust rose into a fog when disturbed, making work even more treacherous. Sub-terrestrial gravity hindered solid footing and precise movements, but did not reduce equipment inertia. Progress was a tedious balancing act helped by handholds and cables strung between the module and the complex.

Despite his suit's air conditioning, Joe began to sweat. He paused and stared out at the slight curve of the irregular horizon. Beyond was a dazzling sea of stars and the bottomless black of space. He moved to the loose talon and positioned the chisel. It would take several minutes to prepare the rock for a temporary grapple. He would secure the talon when the proper drill bits arrived.

ROY STOOD IN the tube corridor outside the office airlock and stared at the breach. An icon on his helmet display flashed red, indicating no air in the tube, a fact already made clear by the elliptical hole. He went through the main complex airlock into the hallway. The corridor emergency lights were on, and a length of string tied to a duct grating waved in the airflow. He stopped outside the rec room where a wall display showed normal air pressure and temperature inside. He peered through the hatch window into an empty room. His helmet's atmosphere icon now showed a steady green. He took off his S3 helmet and wiped the sweat from his forehead. Stopping outside the dorm unit, Roy looked through the hatch window and saw Bhani sitting on her bunk and Floyd in a chair next to her. He opened the dorm hatch and stood in the doorway.

"Roy, what happened?" she asked.

"A breach in the front tube."

"Any idea what caused it?"

"Not clear yet. Floyd, you, Bhani, and Julio start the repair, and I'll help as soon as I can."

IN THE MODULE, Ved paced back and forth, inspecting displays.

"Get an update on the crew."

Jeff worked his console.

"They're repairing the breach. Julio inspected the complex and found no more damage."

"Where is the breach?"

"On the backside of the office corridor."

"Are the crew all OK?"

Jeff nodded. "Yup. All present and no injuries."

"Get Lauren on the horn."

Jeff tapped some console buttons.

"Hello, Dr. Chen? This is Jeff Mullen in the module. Ved would like to speak with you."

"OK Jeff. Put him on."

"Lauren, what happened?"

"Ved, early this morning, a breach occurred in the tube connecting the office to the mine complex. We're calling it a meteorite strike."

"Calling it a meteorite strike? What else might we call it?"

"That depends."

"On what?"

"Ved, come look at it, then you tell me what to call it."

Ved looked at Jeff and shook his head. "And down the rabbit hole we go."

MOST OF THE mine complex was below the asteroid's surface. The entrance and office sat at ground level with an exposed exterior wall. Rock walls and overhead shielded the staff from most radiation, and the top supported the antenna array. The office provided workstations and personal quarters for Roy and Lauren. Its windows gave views of the landing area, tube corridor, and two cargo bay doors opening into the rock. The designers argued that exterior cams were safer than windows, but a psychologist claimed windows would be better for staff morale.

The main entrance hatch was on the short exterior tube corridor connecting the office to the mine complex. Staff kept the exposed corridor pressurized for convenience and to reduce airlock wear. With few reasons to go outside, the exterior hatch saw little use. There wasn't much out there except rock, toxic and corrosive dust, radiation, and infinite cold. But there was that view, and every once in a while, they went outside to gaze up in silent reverie. Now the corridor was without atmosphere. The interior airlocks at the corridor's ends had closed when the corridor lost air pressure. The corridor had been a subject of controversy during the design phase. Some had argued against it, fearing what had just occurred. However, as subsequent events proved, its absence could have led to far worse consequences.

The complex was at war with the perpetual enemies of electromechanical and electronic systems. Friction, vibration, heat-flux stress, extreme temperatures, and corrosion, both galvanic and from various gasses and condensates, all took their toll. Surface gear also suffered from the electromagnetic and particle radiation that bombarded the asteroid. The rock overhead provided some protection, but crew time on site was tracked and limited.

VED LOOKED OUT a module window and saw light from the office. He switched on the desk comm.

"Lauren, are there any other breaches?"

The module's wall speaker crackled.

"Ved, it doesn't look like it. We're not seeing any significant air pressure anomalies now, but I'm assuming there could be more breaches. We're reading normal or near normal air pressure in all compartments except the breached corridor. The breach is three meters away from the complex."

"How bad is it?"

"You should come over."

LOGAN AWOKE AND saw Avala gazing down at him. She wore a bright flowered sari, her sapphire braids tied back with a bandanna.

He sat up, rubbing his face. "Sorry, I just conked out."

"I thought I'd better see if you'd gotten lost again. There's a dining area downstairs. See you there in a few." She turned and left the room.

He washed his face, then took the stairs to the atrium. Avala was reading a tablet and using chopsticks to eat from a bowl. She looked up, gave him an appraising once-over, and smiled, dimples appearing on either side of her violet lips.

Logan sat in the empty chair and looked at the bowl of stew, tableware, and another pair of chopsticks set before it. Grabbing the fork, he took a tentative bite.

"Mmm ... not bad. Thank you. For all of this."

She waved absently. "No thanks necessary. You're going to earn it."

He set down his fork. "I have to ask. Why did you choose those mods?"

"Which ones?"

"All of them. The eyes, skin, hair."

"Why not?"

"I don't know. I've seen few people go to that extreme."

Avala shrugged. "I like them." She took a bite from her bowl.

"Does anyone live in the apartments upstairs?"

"Not anymore." She picked at her food with the chopsticks.

"You're here by yourself?"

"Not all the time. Why do you ask?"

"I'm just curious about you and this place."

She set down her chopsticks and dabbed her lips with a napkin.

"Careful. You know what they say about curiosity and the cat."

He sat back, folded his arms, and looked at her with raised eyebrows.

"And you don't think I'm smarter than a cat."

She gazed at him, a smirk playing at the corners of her lips.

"That remains to be seen."

His eyes narrowed over a sly grin.

"You've got some kind of nerve. You think you can get away with that? Out with it, now. This place is ..."

She pointed around the room with a blue index finger.

"This lab was built for staff working on environmental remediation and terraforming. They also consulted on stationary and pelagic habitat design and construction. At peak activity, a dozen staff lived and worked here. When the projects were done, they moved on, and sector admin auctioned the place off."

Logan nodded with approval. "See? That wasn't so hard. Who owns the place now?"

"I do." She turned her attention to her bowl.

"How did you get financing, if I'm not being too nosy?"

She looked up, her emerald-green eyes shifting out the window overlooking the verdant forest.

"You are being too nosy."

He set his bowl down. "Look, Avala, if we're going to work together, we have to communicate, and we have to trust each other."

"You're right, Logan. I bought the lab at auction using a loan from my previous employer. So, what about you? What did you do before starting your business?"

"I grew up on Mars orbitals. My father was a structural engineer, and my mother worked in admin. I went to Earth for college but dropped out after my junior year."

"Why did you quit?"

"I got a summer internship with the Pacifica revenue service, and it took over my life."

"That sounds interesting. What did you do?"

Logan swirled his fork and took a bite.

"I worked on a team tracking down tax cheats. I did the research and IT work, then made arrests with two ex-military hard asses."

Her green eyes widened. "That sounds dangerous."

He shrugged. "It wasn't. I just went along to explain the technical stuff and read them their rights. Most of the deadbeats curled up into fetal balls when they saw the muscle. Those two guys were ugly scary. So, what about your background?"

"Before I came here, I worked at an R and D firm in information services. Hydroponics is a hobby."

"Tech and biology. That's an interesting combination."

"I like variety, which is one reason I left that firm and moved here."

"What company was that?"

She gazed at him for a moment.

"Pelitat Corporation."

He shook his head and took a bite from his bowl. "Never heard of it."

"No, you wouldn't have. They keep a low profile."

Logan set down his fork, wiped his lips, then examined her.

And you do too, blue lady. I wonder what you've got under those violet fingernails.

Checking the wall clock, she got up and rinsed her bowl in the sink.

"Meet me back here in an hour. We've got work to do. You're about to earn your keep."

MAGDI STRODE DOWN the corridor and into the Alpha Zubrin board meeting room. Walking in, he buttoned his jacket and shot his cuffs. He looked around at the sitting board members, all facing two seats. One was empty, and the other occupied by the corpulent Bernie Grant, who squirmed and glared at Magdi.

Bernie scowled at the board president. "What's he doing here?"

The president nodded to Magdi and gestured to the empty chair next to Bernie.

"Dr. El-Said, please, have a seat."

Magdi unbuttoned his jacket and sat, ignoring Bernie, who began turning pink, sweat beading on his forehead.

The president cleared his throat.

"Dr. El-Said, we're here to address concerns voiced by Mr. Grant and to plan a proper course of action." Bernie's squirming increased as the board turned its collective gaze on him. "Mr. Grant, now that we're all here, please explain your concerns."

"He's mismanaging the operations division," Bernie said, pointing at Magdi. "He's wasting resources and not generating the returns he should be."

Magdi raised his eyebrows at Bernie.

"Dr. El-Said, we'd like your input," the president said.

Magdi gazed at Bernie.

"Bernie, please be specific. Let's start with 'wasting resources'. What, exactly, are the resources I'm wasting?"

"You're wasting money on staff training boondoggles and compensation schemes."

"Boondoggles and schemes? Really? I didn't get a copy of your report, Bernie, the one you distributed to the board before this meeting. You did distribute such a report, did you not?"

A bead of sweat broke free from a wrinkle on Bernie's forehead and streamed down a cheek.

Magdi's eyes narrowed. "Please, Bernie, show us your data."

The board members glanced at each other, then at the president.

Bernie cleared his throat. "The report's not yet finalized."

Magdi nodded in amusement, then addressed the board.

"Well, I do have data. For those of you not familiar with my division, let me start with a summary of our overall philosophy regarding staff training and compensation." He took his tablet from a jacket pocket and tapped several icons. The display on the boardroom wall came to life with a page showing his division's revenue report for the previous year, along with the number of patents filed.

"There are reasons our division leads the industry in innovation and productivity. We hire the best people in the business. We treat them as what they are: respected colleagues and peers. We compensate them very well, and we offer them as many opportunities for professional development as they desire. But perhaps

Bernie would prefer we invest that money in stock buy-backs. I'm sure that would better serve his personal interests, right, Bernie?"

"You're running some kind of skunk-works over there."

"And since you're here, Bernie, I'd like to bring up the business of you harassing my staff."

"I'm doing no such thing!"

"That's interesting, Bernie, because I'm hearing different from my people. Apparently, you've been trying to get classified information from them. I've gotten reports of you attempting to intimidate R and D and mining staff. Several of them are upset, and some have told me they're updating their resumes." Magdi shifted his gaze to the board. "AZ can't afford to lose good people."

The president adjusted his mic.

"Dr. El-Said, we presume you have evidence of this."

Magdi nodded. "I'll forward copies of my staff's signed affidavits to all of you. Please, let me continue."

He turned his gaze back to Bernie.

"You spread rumors undermining division credibility and leadership. You talk about others wasting resources while you scheme, connive, and make unsupported charges against me and my people."

Bernie's sweating was now profuse.

"You and your people! A bunch of pampered, overpaid prima donnas is what you are!"

Magdi folded his arms and stared at Bernie.

"I wasn't aware of your management expertise, Bernie. Did you get it from all those bankruptcies? How much longer before daddy's money runs out?"

His eyes bulging, Bernie's complexion turned a deep red.

"Why, you arrogant little shit!"

The board's reaction ranged from amusement to horrified shock.

Magdi stiffened, then sat up and turned in his chair, staring hard at Bernie.

The board president inspected the other members. One raised his hand, and the president nodded.

"Mr. President, I've seen no evidence supporting Grant's claims. I move we dismiss the issue. I have more pressing work, as do the rest of us."

"Alright, all in favor of dismissing the issue before this body, raise your hands."

The vote was unanimous, and everyone rose from their chairs.

Bernie mopped sweat from his face and glared at the podium in silence. He avoided eye contact with Magdi, who stood and stared at him while buttoning his suit jacket. Magdi then straightened his tie, shot his cuffs, and walked toward the door as Bernie shuffled to the refreshments table.

He exited the boardroom and glanced at Magdi, leaning against the far wall, his arms folded.

"Bernie, would you care to continue our discussion in the athletic center? Your choice of weapons."

He pretended to not hear Magdi and headed up the corridor.

"Bernie, the athletic center's that way," Magdi called out after him, pointing in the opposite direction. "Come on, Bernie. You must outweigh me by ... what? Three hundred pounds? Let's settle this like men."

5

TERZAKIAN STRODE DOWN the security office corridor, then turned into Spencer's office and stopped in front of his desk. Spencer looked up from a tablet, his face tightening into a hostile stare. Terzakian looked down at him.

"You went around me and ordered my subordinate to act illegally."

Spencer stared back with jaw-jutting defiance.

"I saw you on the security cams. You had that puke in the bone-yard, but you let him go. He was wanted for unauthorized access of facilities, trespassing, and theft."

"There's no evidence of that, but if there was, we'd have brought him in peacefully. He was unarmed and harmless, but you ordered Mahon to shoot him."

"I did no such thing."

Terzakian stared at him. "I know my people, Spencer, and they say different."

"You have no proof."

"You were trying to set up my man to absorb blow-back. I've seen that kind of thing before."

Spencer gave him a puzzled look. "Why do you care so much, anyhow?"

"If you really have to ask that question, then you wouldn't understand my answer."

Spencer attempted a bland gaze up at Terzakian, but the effect failed.

Terzakian braced his palms on the desktop and leaned forward.

"I've seen men like you before, Spencer. I've seen the damage they can do. I don't care what rank you hold; if you pull another stunt like that, I'll bring you up on charges. My men and I are ready to testify in court." He straightened and backed away from Spencer's desk. "You've wasted too much of my time already, and I'm only going to say this once: stay away from my people, and stay away from me."

Terzakian turned and headed to the door.

"What's your problem?" Spencer yelled after him. "Why are you such a problem?"

Terzakian paused at the door and looked over his shoulder.

"I don't know, Spencer. Maybe my mother didn't breastfeed me long enough."

TERZAKIAN WAS IN the ready room when his pocket comm buzzed. He stared at the display.

FROM: B. SPENCER, Director, Zandax/Marsh Security

TO: A. TERZAKIAN

AS OF 1800 TODAY, YOUR SERVICES AT MARSH CORPORATION ARE NO LONGER REQUIRED. REMOVE ALL PERSONAL ITEMS FROM THE FACILITY AND VACATE THE PREMISES BY 1900.

YOUR SEVERANCE PAY WILL BE CREDITED TO YOUR ACCOUNT.

JULIO, BHANI, AND Floyd sat in the rec room staring at the images on the wall display.

"Julio, did you show these to Roy yet?"

"No, Bhani. I wanted you and Floyd to see them first. Roy's next."

Floyd shook his head and stared at the display.

"Wow. Has Roy said anything about the hole in the tube?"

"No, just patching instructions."

"Apparently, it was cut by whoever left those tracks in the mine dust. That black thing in the vent chamber looks like a tank or a container. I'll bet there's something interesting in it."

Bhani folded her arms and looked at them.

"I wonder who did this, and why? It's safe to say no one from AZ."

Floyd nodded. "They may come back. Maybe they're still here."

"And what will they do next?" Bhani asked.

Julio fidgeted and looked at the clock. "I'll get Roy's take on this."

JULIO TAPPED ON Roy's office hatch frame. He looked up from his console and pointed to the empty seat by his desk.

"Julio, you didn't follow my instruction to stay put earlier."

"I apologize for that, Roy. I found something you need to see."

He took his tablet from a pocket, tapped the interface, and the wall display refreshed. The images began with the footprints in the dust. It was too dangerous for staff to go where the robotic machinery operated; the risk of cave-ins or sink-holes was too great. Unless mine staff had been sleep-walking, the footprints over the machinery tracks were not theirs.

Roy looked at the images and whistled softly.

"We know whoever cut the hole in the tube walked into the mine. Next question: what is that black structure in the vent chamber? What does the crew think?"

"We're all curious and worried."

Roy nodded. "Lauren has to see these. But let's discuss your actions this morning."

"Again, Roy, I'm sorry. I—"

"Never mind that. My point here is what I'm about to ask of you. First, let's review skill sets. Bhani and Floyd are university-educated engineers. They're long on academic theory, but right now, short on field experience. Joe is the opposite: an old hand, long on field experience, but with little theoretical background."

"Well, Roy, I'm at the bottom of that totem pole."

"I'm talking about a different totem pole, Julio."

"I don't follow."

"You have a fresh perspective, calm under pressure, and the ability to assert rational, organized action in a crisis."

"Roy, if you're referring to Africa, all that proves is that I was lucky. One thing I've learned is to not rely on luck."

"And that's part of it. This morning, you showed initiative and courage in acting to assess a potentially dire threat. I want you running point on the crew. Report to me and Lauren. Are you OK with that?"

"I'll do whatever is necessary, Roy."

"Good. Go see Lauren and bring her up to speed; show her what you've just shown me."

JULIO, SCRUBBED AND wearing clean overalls, eased into the mine office and looked around.

"Dr. Chen, Roy asked me to show you some images I got from the mine."

"Have a seat, Julio. I'm not big on titles, so just call me Lauren. What have you got?"

He handed her his cam, and she linked the unit to her console. As she scrolled the images on the display, her eyes widened.

"Did you show these to anyone else?"

"Yes. Besides Roy, the crew has seen them."

Lauren downloaded the images to her workstation, then handed the cam back to Julio.

"What are their thoughts on this?"

"For starters, they're worried about who made the breach and if they're coming back."

She scrolled the images and paused at the black structure in the vent chamber. "What is that?"

"That's one of the questions."

"OK. The intruder is involved with that black structure. Ved needs to see these."

She put on a headset and thumbed the mic button.

"Ved, I need you over here." She looked at Julio. "To be continued."

Julio nodded and left the office.

Zubie trotted over and hopped into Lauren's lap. She stroked his head and stared at the display.

IN THE MODULE, Ved scrolled through environmental and structural data for Asteroid 2060RT2. Because of its size, Lauren called it a dwarf planet, although others avoided that designation. They claimed it would attract undesirable attention to a lucrative asset. Ved looked at data on what appeared to be gas vents in the asteroid's interior. Then he looked at the mine environmental logs. Immediately after the breach, a pattern of minor air pressure anomalies appeared, likely caused by a sequence of hatches opening and closing.

Ved switched to a broadcast channel known to be monitored by corporate snoops and then spoke in a loud, clearly articulated voice.

"Lauren, Ved here. We're done, so let's wrap it up and go home."

Jeff looked at him with raised eyebrows.

Ved gave him a conspiratorial wink, then shut off the comm.

"Your report will be simple, Jeff. The complex suffered a minor meteorite strike, and the damage has been repaired. There were no injuries, and normal operations will resume tomorrow morning."

Jeff's eyes narrowed, and then he nodded. "Well, alrighty then, Dr. Ved. I'll schedule the shuttle."

Ved inspected several displays.

"Jeff, let's keep the module here for research on the breach. Say we're getting data for the materials improvement program."

"OK. I'll send Magdi a status report requesting more resources. I'll lock down all network comm channels out of here, and if anyone squawks, just mumble about proprietary engineering stuff we don't want the competition getting hold of."

"I knew I made a good choice giving you a spot on this project."

"Yeah, but it's not clear I did by accepting."

Ved took off his headset. "I'm going over to talk with Lauren. I'll be back in an hour or two."

VED WENT TO the airlock and switched on his personal comm. "Lauren, I'm on my way over." He put on an S3, went into the airlock, and worked the control panels. Hatches hissed open and shut, and he stepped out onto the asteroid's surface. He clipped onto the safety line and went to the office as Lauren watched him through a window. He cleared the mine airlocks, then removed his S3 and stepped into the office.

Lauren looked up at him.

"I got an interesting report from Julio with images you'll want to see." She pointed at a display.

Ved stared at it and shook his head. "Obvious question: who cut that hole?"

"And why?"

"I've got some interesting data from system records. Where's Roy? What's his take on this?"

"He's checking equipment and infrastructure. He asked Julio to bring us up to speed."

"What about the rest of the crew? What's their thinking?"

"I don't know for sure, but Julio said they're worried about the hole, who cut it, and what it means for our safety. After the breach, Julio checked the entire complex. He saw nothing unusual until he went into the mine. And there are more images. You might want to sit down."

The display refreshed, showing images of Julio's progress as he followed the intruder's footprints in the dust. The images showed many irregular openings in the mine corridors, presumably gas vents formed from magma millions of years earlier. Most vents petered out into a filigree of tiny holes, but some continued for unknown distances into the asteroid's crust. An image showed a disturbance in the dust at a vent entrance opened by the boring machine. The next one showed Julio's sketch of his route, then a close-up of the chamber entrance. When Ved saw the last image, he sat down and stared at the black structure.

VED, LAUREN, AND Roy were sitting at the conference table and staring at the display when the airlock hatch hissed. Julio, Bhani, Joe, and Floyd walked in and took the empty chairs, and for a moment, they all just looked at one another.

Ved cleared his throat. "We need to discuss a few things."

Lauren looked around the group. "Ved has a talent for understatement."

"You've all seen Julio's cam images," he said. "First, we need a threat assessment. Roy?"

"OK. Let's start with the fact that the breach was carefully done. The intruder removed the hull section as cleanly as possible, and there's no further damage anywhere that we've found. I think that tells us a lot."

Julio raised an index finger.

"Don't forget the lock pad scratches. I think they tried to come in through the front hatch, but couldn't open it."

Ved looked at Roy. "What about security cam footage?"

"This facility has no wall cams. They weren't included in the site spec. Joe, can we get any security cam clips from the module?"

"No, the docking area activity raised too much dust. We can't get decent images at that distance."

Ved caught Roy's eye. "Any idea what that structure in the vent chamber is?

"No. It doesn't look like anything used in mining operations, no technology I'm aware of. And it's not clear how it got in that chamber. Ved, I'm getting a strange feeling about this."

Ved looked around the group. "What action does the evidence call for?"

Bhani raised her hand.

"I don't think our visitor intends any harm. They had the opportunity last night. The chamber images make me think they will return, and we should stay out of their way.

Roy looked at her. "Go on."

"Well, there are six openings on the structure's top, two uncapped and four capped. I think we've caught them in the middle of a procedure."

"And I think they intend to complete that procedure," Floyd said.

Joe looked at them with raised eyebrows.

"So, why don't we just let them? Leave the front hatch open tonight. They apparently know how to operate the airlocks, and I don't want to patch another hull breach."

Julio nodded. "And given their obvious ability, I don't think trying to stop them would be wise."

Ved looked at Joe. "Do we have any portable security cams?"

"No, but I think I can cobble one together from spare parts."

Bhani frowned and shook her head.

"We should think twice about that. If our visitor sees it, there could be unintended consequences. I don't think we should risk interfering with their procedure."

Ved nodded. "Valid point. Joe, let's hold off on installing that cam, but get it ready." He looked at the group. "Any other immediate concerns or input?"

Lauren raised an index finger.

"Viewing the evidence, we may have to consider something I hesitate to bring up."

"I think I know what you're suggesting," Julio said. "And it would sound crazy, but ... Roy?"

"AZ would have a hard time swallowing a story about aliens, but I'm ready for retirement. Hell, I'll say it and let them yell and scream all they want. I would enjoy going out on an exciting note."

Ved shook his head. "Given interstellar distances, the probability would be infinitesimal."

"According to our science and technology."

"Good point, Lauren. OK. But let's assume a Sol System organization is behind the intrusion and the objects. Evacuating the site will green-light looting. If we stay, thieves might think twice before coming here. They won't know that we're unarmed, so I don't think they'll risk a confrontation."

"I hope you're right, Ved," Roy said.

Ved looked at the group.

"Keep this under wraps until we know more. Network security is uncertain, so no outgoing comm traffic. We can't risk an information leak. I'll go to Hawkington to talk with Magdi. We can proceed from there. Start working on the assumption we'll be shutting the site down, but don't do anything irreversible before

I get back. The repair module can stay here for your use. Anyone wanting to leave now can go with me on the shuttle or catch it when I come back. Who wants to stay?"

Everyone raised their hands.

Ved's eyes widened. "Really?" He looked at Floyd. "Why?"

"For me, that's easy. Stubborn hillbilly curiosity."

"OK, everybody go eat and get some rest."

FLOYD SAT NURSING a beer and staring at the rec room display. In a corner, Joe was working out on a resistance trainer, the hissing of his expelled breaths punctuating the silence. Bhani was sitting in a chair, twisting a strand of hair absently and examining her tablet. Julio leaned against the wall and looked around the room.

Finished with his workout, Joe used his T-shirt to wipe sweat from his head and neck. He pulled a beer from the refrigerator and studied the can.

"If the rest of the week is like today, we'll need a lot more of these."

Julio nodded and walked to the kitchen area. "I'll start chow going." Bhani went to help him.

Roy came in and leaned against the kitchen counter. Bhani caught his eye.

"What's the plan, Roy?"

"Hunker down here until I buzz you tomorrow morning. Keep your S3s and comms handy. The front hatch will be open, so no tube corridor traffic tonight unless there's an emergency. Questions?"

The crew looked at him and shook their heads.

"Buzz me if you have any." He turned and left the room.

Joe looked around. "Anyone planning to sleep tonight?"

Floyd nodded. "We should at least try."

Julio fetched a beer, took a sip, and looked at them.

"I don't want to spend the next twelve hours thinking about how this could go sideways on us."

"But you probably will, Julio."

"Bhani, you know me too well."

Joe pointed to a gray box on a side table.

"For a distraction, the entertainment console has a great selection of movies."

He tapped a console button, and the display lit up with a title:

It! The Terror from Beyond Space

Floyd shook his head. "And you guys call me a smart-ass."

Joe grinned at him. "I figure you can use some help."

Bhani smiled at Joe. "A movie sounds very nice. You pick it."

IN THE EVENING, Avala and Logan sat on the terrace and watched the chattering tree creatures scamper about in the foliage. Logan leaned back in his chair and put his feet up on the railing.

"Tell me more about this place."

"This lab was built for a consortium of scientists, engineers, and businesses working on new habitat designs. After making many important technical advances, design improvements, and a lot of money, they drifted off to other projects. After they left, the lab was vacant, and it's perfect for me. So I bought it, and here I am."

Logan regarded the tiny feathered creature perched on his leg, then looked at her.

"I wonder what those people were like. Did you know any of them?"

"I knew one when she was nearing the end of her life. She faced the questions we all will face. What did her life mean? Did it ultimately serve any purpose?"

Logan gazed at her for a moment, then at the little creature clambering up his shirt and onto his shoulder.

"Meaning and purpose. Those are rather thorny, but I think I understand them for myself." He shrugged in response to her quizzical look. "There is no meaning or purpose. We just are. Until we aren't anymore. So, what did she conclude?"

The creature hopped from Logan's shoulder onto hers and played with her earring until she gave it a treat. It took the offering, then jumped onto the railing and raced up into the nearest tree.

Avala regarded Logan for a moment.

"She concluded her work had made other people's lives better, and she was at peace."

6

VED'S SHUTTLE DOCKED at the elevator terminal. Stationed several kilometers above the Martian surface, it served AZ's low-gravity manufacturing facility. A product of nanotube technology, it provided efficient transport to and from Hawkington. Fifteen minutes later, Ved strode into the Alpha Zubrin complex.

Hawkington's surface structures and the exotic Martian terrain inspired humility in most visitors. Its geodesic domes were transparent enough between supports to provide an awe-inspiring view of the Martian sky, its two moons, and beyond. The dome material allowed the weak Martian sunlight to warm the interiors while blocking dangerous radiation. It also reflected long wavelengths back into the domes, reducing radiant heat loss.

Ved crossed the docking area to the administrative complex with his usual brisk, purposeful stride. He nodded curtly to the receptionist and marched straight into Magdi's office, stopping at the edge of the huge, highly polished oak desk.

Magdi looked up from his console. He picked up a stylus and began twiddling it through his fingers.

"Ved, come right on in."

Magdi stood, and they walked to a pair of easy chairs in a

corner. Giving Ved a conspiratorial wink, he pointed around the room and then at his ears, placing an index finger across his lips. Ved nodded in understanding.

"Things are going well, Magdi. Everything is on schedule. I'm here to check some items in the engineering lab." He pointed toward the door, and Magdi nodded.

"Great. Let's go on over."

They strolled out into the corridor. When they were a few meters past the office entrance, Ved looked at Magdi.

"Who do you think is bugging your office?"

"The usual ambitious or jealous players with too much time on their hands. I use their bugs to feed them bullshit, but I'm not in the mood right now." He gave Ved a once-over. "OK, I know that look. Let's have it."

Ved pulled his tablet from a jacket pocket and handed it to Magdi.

"An intruder has been coming into the mine after hours. We don't know who, or what."

Magdi gave him a puzzled look.

"Or what?"

He scrolled Ved's images, then stopped walking and stared at the tablet.

Ved pointed at the screen.

"Look at how that tube section was removed. When the tube depressurized, the breach alarm woke the staff. That's the only damage, and nothing is missing. We have no idea what that black structure in the vent chamber is. Lauren's working on it. Until we know more, I think it's too risky for staff to continue normal operations. We don't know what we're dealing with."

Magdi stared at the tablet.

"That black structure must be related to the breach. No competitor did this, not with our staff there."

"Lauren's looking for ongoing projects we haven't heard of yet. It may be trespass, or ..."

"Or what?"

"Magdi, let's close the site until we get a handle on this. You know what'll happen if word gets out."

Magdi closed his eyes and shook his head.

"This will raise hell with our production schedule. I can just hear the board yelling and screaming."

"Louder than they'll yell and scream when we try to explain injured, missing, or dead staff?"

Magdi inspected Ved.

"You're genuinely rattled. I never thought I'd see the day. How bad do you think this could get?"

"As bad as we let it get. Lauren tried to analyze the structure's material with her portable equipment, but got no results. Her gear has always worked with anything made from known technology. So, use your imagination."

Ved studied him with a raised eyebrow, and Magdi gave him a sideways look.

"Are you suggesting what I think you're suggesting?"

"What do you think I'm suggesting?"

"A non-Sol System entity."

Ved gave Magdi a sly look. "Aliens?"

"I don't like where this is going."

"I don't either. Where do you want it to go?"

"What do you propose?"

"I'll help Lauren write a report concluding the site's a dry hole. We'll need budget and inventory adjustments, shuttles, and staff reassignments to a secure lab. The mine crew can work there incommunicado. Lauren can scrub the data so the site looks worthless. I'll handle the reports. You just keep the board fat, dumb, and happy."

Magdi handed Ved the tablet, then leaned against the corridor wall and crossed his arms.

"We'll have to convince them the initial survey data were wrong. I can sell it if the new numbers work." His eyes narrowed. "I'll have Lauren give them a presentation while wearing that tight black outfit that makes her look like a venomous spider. It'll help ease the smoke up their asses."

Ved looked around the corridor. It was still empty.

"Rumor is you have a thing for venomous spiders."

Magdi grimaced and rubbed his face.

"And I've got the bites to prove it. How is the mine crew reacting?"

"They understand the situation and aren't panicking. I offered to evacuate them, but they're willing to stay and do the work."

"What are your immediate plans at the site?"

"Julio Ortiz is leading the mine shutdown. That includes packing small valuables and servicing the large machinery for on-site storage. He found the structure in the vent chamber and got the cam images. Lauren and Roy vouch for him. We think the intruder will return, possibly tonight. The crew will avoid contact. I'm going back when we're done here."

Magdi nodded. "Let's continue this in the gym."

They marched off down the corridor, the light Martian gravity putting a bounce in their step.

LOGAN WALKED INTO the lab's data room to find Avala seated at a terminal.

"What's up?"

She smiled at him. "Have a seat. Right now, I'm after data on Alpha Zubrin's asteroid mining. I'd like to see their entire inventory, but that's likely a tad ambitious."

"What's so interesting about Alpha Zubrin's mining operations?"

"Pelitat wants data on Alpha's asteroids. It's considering an arrangement with Alpha to work on those with interesting resources, so it needs information on each asteroid. Pelitat's negotiating position will be better if it has this information in advance. I think getting it on the sly might help."

"Do you mind if I poke around a bit?"

"I'll welcome any help I can get."

Logan sat at a terminal and browsed the lab's data system. He found a small icon embedded in a string of numbers. It opened a workspace on his display, and he scrolled through the contents.

"Is this some kind of encryption?"

Avala looked over his shoulder at the moving text, then pulled up a chair.

"An English phonetic transliteration of random sequences of technical acronyms from several languages. The target's decryption system analyzes series of images and symbols, then uses their distributions to create English characters."

He gave her a rueful frown. "Seriously?"

She nodded. "The target's supposed to think that's information and try to decrypt it. I thought I deleted all the links in this file."

"The target?"

"Of that stuff. It's a hoax to show how gullible the target's people are, before I break into their system."

"Does it work?"

"It did, but I'm sure word got out, so I don't use it anymore. The rest of that file just contains assorted flaky fantasies. But never mind that for now."

"How were they supposed to find it? Did you plant the file?"

"I broadcast it on an obscure sub-frequency when I knew their staff would be looking. I predicted, correctly—"

"Of course," Logan interjected with a note of sanctimony.

Avala cleared her throat and flashed him a scowl.

"As I was saying, I predicted correctly they would be too busy congratulating themselves on finding it to notice how silly it was."

Her fingers played over the virtual console, and the scrolling text disappeared. She looked around, her eyes reflecting stray flashes of light from a hydroponic tank, as if searching for something beyond her field of vision.

"I need more information,"

UNABLE TO SLEEP, Lauren was in the mine office, catching up on document work, when her concentration failed. She retreated to her bunk and drifted into a semi-conscious state. Zubie began growling, then shot off the bed and bolted into the closet. She sat up and glanced at her bedside clock: 02:43.

"Mister Zubie, what's the matter, little boy?"

Lauren looked out the window. In the starlight, she saw the surrounding area and the gray tube corridor connecting to the complex; there was no further damage. Half-asleep, she sat and gazed at the exotic landscape.

"It's OK, Zubie, you can come out now."

The cat did not budge.

FLOYD AWOKE IN the rec room's dim light. Raising his recliner, he stood and stretched. In another chair, Joe slept, his breathing slow and steady. Bhani and Julio had gone back to their bunks. Floyd looked at the wall clock; its display showed 03:51. He stepped into the kitchen area and started a pot of coffee.

Bhani and Julio sat on his bunk as Roy's voice came over Julio's comm.

"Listen up. Stay in the dorm until I give the OK. Please acknowledge."

"OK, Roy. We'll wait here for your instructions."

Lauren sat up to the tapping on her stateroom door.

"Lauren, it's Roy. The system monitor picked up those same air pressure anomalies again. Our visitor may be back. Sit tight, and I'll keep you posted."

ONE HUNDRED METERS away, Ved and Jeff sat at the module's console bank. Jeff, still in his underwear, brought up the images of Lauren and Roy on a display.

"Roy, check system data and get back to me ASAP. Wait an hour then have Julio do an inspection."

"OK, Ved."

"When he's back, start damage repair, but don't patch breaches until I see them. I'll be there soon."

"Got it."

"Prepare another facility report when Julio's finished his check."

"OK, Ved. Anything else?"

"A lot else, Roy, but I think you've got enough for now."

Roy disconnected then brought up system data on the displays.

AN HOUR LATER, Roy told Julio to inspect the complex and report to the office. Julio put on his S3 while Bhani, Floyd, and Joe looked at the display showing corridor atmosphere data. The pressure and temperature readings were normal.

"OK, see you in a while." Julio opened the hatch and stepped into the corridor.

He walked past the rec room to the tube corridor airlock. The vestibule's hatch display showed normal atmosphere inside. He punched the open key, stepped into the vestibule, and the hatch slid shut. The transit chamber was next. When it finished charging, Julio opened the hatch and stepped in. The system evacuated the transit chamber, processing and storing the air. When this last operation was done, Julio opened the final airlock hatch and stepped into the tube corridor. He switched on his flashlight and looked to his left. The tube wall was intact; there was no new breach. To his right, the front hatch was closed. He spoke into his suit comm.

"Roy, there's no damage, but someone closed the front hatch. I assume you didn't do it."

"Correct, Julio. Earlier this morning, the system monitor picked up another pattern of air pressure anomalies. I think our visitor's had enough time to finish their business, so go check that vent chamber. If you see any sign of their presence—"

"Then I'll set a new world record for sprinting in an S3."

LAUREN WAS SITTING with her tablet when Ved came into the office. He studied the worn and guarded expression clouding her features as she drummed her fingernails on the table. He joined her, and they sat together in silent thought.

Fifteen minutes later, Julio and Roy came in and Lauren looked up.

"What did you find?"

Julio linked his cam to a console, then scrolled a series of images on the display. Ved and Lauren stared at the structure in the vent chamber. Two more cells were uncapped, leaving two remaining.

Roy looked at Lauren and Ved.

"The only signs of intrusion this morning are more air pressure anomalies, Julio's new images, and the closed front hatch. I'm going to pressurize the front tube."

Lauren watched Roy leave, then resumed drumming her fingernails on the tabletop. She shifted her gaze to Ved. "They'll probably come tonight to get what's in those last two cells."

"And I hope that ends this business, but it may not. Why didn't they use the front hatch before? Why go to the other side and cut a hole?"

Julio caught Ved's eye.

"They tried the front hatch's open button, hence the scratch. They knew they couldn't open the coded lock, so no scratches there. When the button didn't work, they went with Plan B."

Lauren nodded. "Our visitor likely knew the module staff could see them at the front hatch. The view is clear when the dust settles."

Julio raised an index finger.

"Also, the tube is easier to cut than a hatch and easier to repair, if that's a consideration."

Ved stood and stretched.

"OK, let's continue winding things down here and assume there will be another visit early tomorrow morning. We'll handle it the same way we did today."

JOE, BHANI, FLOYD, and Julio sat around the central rec room table, finishing the evening meal in silence.

Joe looked at the group. "You guys are sure quiet tonight. I haven't heard a peep out of Floyd."

Floyd looked at him. "Having the bejesus scared out of me tends to do that. Julio, did you find anything more in the vent system?"

"No, but I didn't go very far. I'm pretty sure there are more chambers back there, but I'm not in a particularly adventurous mood just now."

Bhani looked at Julio with mock surprise.

"Gosh, why not? Where's your sense of curiosity, your sense of adventure?"

Julio shook his head and grinned at her.

"Right now, mamacita, both are pretty much used up. My curiosity is down to how soon we can get off this rock."

Joe gave him a thumbs-up.

"If there are more of those big black boxes here, the visitor will probably be back. What if they decide we're too much of a risk to their operation?"

Bhani shook her head. "I don't feel like sticking around to find out."

"If it was up to me," Joe said, "we'd be having a cold one in the Hawkington Tap Room."

Floyd looked around. "So, they came for something in that black box and just waltzed right in without so much as a by-your-leave. Who has that kind of brass?"

Joe shook his head. "None of our competitors that I'm aware of."

"I'd like to look in those capped cells," Julio said, "but something tells me it would be a bad idea. Brace yourselves for a third visit tonight or early tomorrow. Same plan: lie low until the visitor leaves."

Floyd nodded. "And hope they leave for good."

Julio looked at the group.

"Lauren suggested something earlier today, but she said the call was ours. Bhani made a good point about Joe's cam possibly spooking our visitor, but what do you think about me installing it in the vent chamber tonight? This may be our last chance. If the visitor shows up, they will probably clear those last two cells. They may never return, and we'll never know who or what they are. Bhani, what are you thinking?"

"I was indulging in fantasies of a good night's sleep tonight. Silly me. But yes, I think it's a good idea." She looked at Joe and Floyd. "OK?" They both nodded in silent assent.

AT THE USUAL bedtime, Julio returned to his cubicle. He put on his headset and lay back on the bunk. He looked at the shelf by the entertainment display. On it were two small woven straw figures. One was a campesino, the traditional Mexican farmer, the other a burro, the farmer's beast of burden. They had been a gift from his sister Juanita on his twenty-fifth birthday. A bright, multicolored blanket graced the burro's back, and it wore a straw sombrero with holes cut to accommodate its ears. The campesino, dressed in white cotton, sat in mute satisfaction on his docile mount, a bright smile on his tiny brown face. Julio gazed at the straw figures, then went to Bhani's cubicle. He said he was going to install Joe's cam and make an inspection.

Fifteen minutes later, Julio was standing in the mine vent chamber, looking at the black structure. He turned to the rock wall, found a suitable crack, and inserted Joe's cam, a motion-sensitive recorder that could operate without visible light. Then he knelt and retrieved the little straw campesino and his burro from a pouch. He set them on the floor a few centimeters from the black structure, then looked at his small straw friends.

"Vayan con Dios, mis amigos."

JULIO JERKED AWAKE. His nightstand clock showed 05:00. He went to Bhani's cubicle and tapped on the doorframe.

"Did you get any sleep?"

She set down her tablet. "A little. Floyd and Joe were watching movies when I left. I'll see you there in a few minutes."

The crew gathered in the rec room and sat around the table drinking coffee.

"We got a buzz from Roy," Joe said. "Same pattern as yesterday, same procedure today. Wait another hour here before going anywhere."

An hour and fifteen minutes later, Julio stood on the rock

overlooking the structure in the vent chamber. All six cells were now uncapped and empty. Julio's straw figures were gone. In their place was a flat, black object about thirty centimeters across, fifteen centimeters thick, and hexagonal. It appeared to be one of the cell caps. He looked at it for a minute but did not touch it, then he retrieved Joe's cam from the wall crack and returned to the dorm unit.

IN THE MINE office, everyone watched as Lauren inserted the data stick from Joe's cam into the console. The wall display showed a crouching human-like figure in a pressure suit entering through the hole in the chamber wall.

Lauren paused the playback and looked around.

"Does anybody recognize that pressure suit design?"

Roy frowned and shook his head, and Joe shrugged.

Lauren resumed the playback.

The figure inspected the black structure, then removed a collapsible ladder from the back of their pressure suit. They extended the ladder and climbed to the structure's top, then retrieved two cylinders from inside it. After descending the ladder, they attached the items to the back of their suit. They knelt in front of the structure, obscuring the cam's view of what they were doing. A minute later, the figure rose and left the chamber. Without motion, the cam shut off, and the images stopped.

Ved looked around at the group. "What do you all make of this?"

Joe shrugged. "That pressure suit doesn't look like any design I'm aware of."

"I think the visitor could be done with their business here," Bhani said.

Julio nodded. "In that vent chamber. There's something more. The visitor left a cell cap behind. I didn't touch it."

Lauren's eyes widened. "Let's go see it!"

7

TERZAKIAN WALKED TO the Ellis Health and Safety entrance. Inside, a uniformed receptionist motioned him over.

"You must be Mr. Terzakian. The chief's expecting you. Wait one." The door lock buzzed and clicked. The receptionist nodded, and Terzakian walked into the office.

A tall, graying middle-aged man sat behind a cluttered desk.

"I'm Jim Crawford." He rose, and they shook hands.

"Aram Terzakian. Thanks for the interview, sir."

Crawford waved dismissively.

"No need for formalities, Aram. Just call me Jim. I've looked over your resume, and I think we can wrap this up pretty quickly. Just a few questions." He gave Terzakian a curious look. "Can you tell me why you were let go from your previous position?"

Terzakian thought for a second.

"I wasn't given a specific reason, but I had some disagreements with my up line."

"Can you elaborate?"

"When Marsh took over, my job changed in ways I couldn't tolerate. A supervisor gave my squad unlawful orders."

"Can you tell me what they were?"

"Sir, Jim, this must remain confidential."

"Of course."

Terzakian took a moment to gather his thoughts.

"The Marsh up line ordered my squad to seize an unarmed man who had broken no laws. He went around me and ordered my squad member to shoot the man if necessary to apprehend him. I countermanded that order. We had words, and he fired me."

Crawford sat back and studied Terzakian, nodding slowly.

"Alright, Aram, when can you start?"

Terzakian grinned. "Right away sir—Jim. Sorry, some things are just ingrained."

"Apparently, the right things. We have space in the barracks if you need housing."

"I'll take you up on that offer."

Crawford stood. "Alright. Alejandro has paperwork and schedules for training and duty." He pointed to the reception area. "You'll work in firefighting, emergency medical, technical issues, and law enforcement. You're qualified for most, but our bots and systems are new." Crawford extended his hand. "Welcome aboard, Aram."

Terzakian shook it. "Thank you, Jim."

THE ELLIS HEALTH and Safety barracks was a plain, unmarked single-story building with ample windows. Inside, some staff members were in uniform and others in casual clothes. Terzakian walked down the main corridor, looking into open rooms as he passed, and turned into the breakroom. A half-dozen people were talking in small groups or reading. They looked up and made brief eye contact. Some smiled and waved, and one came over and introduced himself.

"Mike Richter. I got word you were coming."

"Aram Terzakian. Just 'Terzakian' works."

"OK. Terzakian, good to meet you. Grab an empty rack in the dorm. The chow hall is in the next corridor. You can get grub any time. If the kitchen staff are out, raid the refrigerator. The rest of these clowns will introduce themselves." He faced the group. "Listen up, weasels. This is our newbie, Aram Terzakian. Don't scare him off like you did the last one."

A chorus of jeers and a shower of wadded food wrappers descended. Mike shook his head, and Terzakian looked around the room and grinned. Several of the staff members were female, young and buffed, and radiating confidence. They made eye contact and nodded. One striking specimen eyed him with frank appraisal, then got up and approached.

"Hana Ramirez." She offered her hand. She had jet-black hair tied in a ponytail, olive skin, generous lips that curved into a beguiling smile, and large brown eyes that missed nothing.

Terzakian smiled and shook her hand.

"Thanks for the welcome, Hana. I'm Aram Terzakian. Just call me Terzakian."

She wore service pants, boots, and a tank top that revealed a vivid and ornate filigree of tattoos over her shoulders and upper arms. He watched the elaborate, multicolored floral patterns move with her muscles, then nodded with approval.

"I like your ink. You'll have to tell me about it sometime."

"My shift is over in a half-hour. Your schedule isn't ready yet, so you have no excuse."

"I'm not one for making excuses."

"Alright then. See you in the lounge in thirty." She strode to a chair, her lean, athletic frame moving with an agile swagger.

A loud male voice sounded.

"Shake it, don't break it!"

She threw the guy a look over her shoulder.

"Stroke it, don't choke it."

An eruption of howls followed.

Terzakian walked to the dorm, stowed his gear, then went to the washroom.

IN THE LOUNGE, Terzakian went to the bar and saw Hana at a table. She caught his eye and waved. He flashed her a grin, then walked over, a cold beer in each hand.

She eyed him and pushed a chair out with her foot.

"Have a seat. You look good out of uniform."

"Thanks. It's nice to hear a kind word for a change."

"I detect a story in there."

"You first." He pointed at her tattoos. "Tell me about that artwork."

"A legacy of my wild youth. I was a problem child." She gave him a wry look and sipped her drink.

"A problem for whom?"

"Mainly for my legal guardians, but for anyone who tried to push me around. So, I got into athletics. A counselor said it would help me 'sublimate my inner tensions'. No shit, she actually said that. OK, your turn."

He leaned back in his chair and looked at the ceiling.

"I grew up in a small town in Oregon. My father worked in

the timber industry, my mother ran the public library. I have a brother and a sister. They went to college while I committed the usual adolescent male blunders. Joined the military right out of high school. Big mistake." He frowned and stared at his drink.

"See any action?"

Nodding, he took a pull on his beer and looked out the lounge window.

"Right out of boot camp. No advanced training. Our unit's first assignment was a combat detail, a bush action that turned into a regular Charlie Foxtrot. On day one, a bunch of guys got killed, and a lot of the wounded later wished they had been. That night, the ring knocker in charge who made the bad calls got fragged in his hooch. The senior NCO got the rest of us out alive after a three-day shit crawl."

She gave him a look of regret. "Sorry. I didn't mean to stir up painful memories."

"It's alright. Sometimes it helps to talk about it. With the right person." He looked her in the eye and raised his bottle in a toast. "To better memories."

She tapped her bottle to his.

"And starting right now." She regarded him with a studied curiosity. "What about after that?"

"I went to work for Zandax security. Only skills I had at that point."

"And here you are. You must like the work."

He shrugged. "Or maybe it's still just the only skill set I have."

"Guess that makes two of us. So here's to us, whose only skills are kicking ass and taking names." They tapped bottles and then took a drink.

He studied her face. "What did you do after school?"

"During the final term, we took an aptitude test. Not clear what good that does a seventeen-year-old. It pegged me as a soldier or a cop. I suffered a failure of the imagination and chose cop."

"From what I've seen, I'd say you made the right call. Where did you start?"

She tapped the table with her index finger. "Right here. Born and raised."

He gave her a wry look. "So, problem child, what are your goals in life?"

She set down her bottle and folded her hands on the table.

"That depends. Short term or long term?"

"Short term."

"That's easy. Chow. I'm starving."

THROUGH THE GLASS atrium wall, Logan saw Avala leaning on the balcony railing. She looked out at the verdant landscape, her violet fingernails contrasting with the railing's smooth white enamel. In nearby tree branches, the feathered squirrel-like creatures scampered and chattered. They approached and gazed at her with large, luminous yellow eyes. Logan went out and stood next to her, watching.

One little creature hopped onto her shoulder, then crept close to her face, reaching out with a tiny, clawed finger to touch her cheek. She fished a grape-sized nutrient lump from her jacket pocket and offered it to the creature. It grabbed the treat and chewed noisily, its sharp-toothed jaws working beneath its multicolored plumage. Then it leaped back into the foliage and disappeared, its tiny companions scampering in noisy pursuit.

Through a light rain, they looked at the expanse of clouded sky above the jungle canopy and the gray habitat wall beyond. Logan's reverie was short-lived as the screeching in the foliage grew louder, and the creatures gathered in a knot on a nearby branch. They sat there, watching him. When he made faces at them, they squeaked and hopped with joy. He looked at Avala, who was eyeing him with a sphinx-like smile.

"What are these little animals?"

"I brought them from my old habitat. I thought they'd make a fun addition to the landscape. The trees provide them with food and shelter. They provide me with protection."

"Protection? From what?"

"Boredom. How did you choose your line of work?"

"I got tired of working for other people, so I started my own consulting business. I put together a resume to show potential clients, listed some technical skills—mostly exaggerated—and figured I'd learn on the job. It's worked well, at least until lately. Most outfits that hire me are clueless, so I can usually do something positive for them. I do things like designing networks, technical troubleshooting, and some financial analyses. My fees are relatively modest, so my conscience is clear. Nobody has successfully sued me yet, so I can't be too far off. At least that's what I keep telling myself. What about you? Any family?"

She straightened up, a surprised look on her face.

"Oh, I just remembered. I have a video appointment in three minutes."

LAUREN AND JULIO stood in the mine vent chamber, looking at the black hexagonal object lying in front of the black structure.

"I didn't touch it," Julio said.

Lauren moved a scanner over it, then she climbed the rock and took images of the structure's top.

"I wonder what those cells contained. That hexagon looks like a cell cap. Why did they leave it?"

"I think it's a gift."

Lauren looked at Julio. "Why?"

"Because I left one for them."

"You did what?"

"I thought a goodwill gesture was in order. I left two woven straw figures, a campesino and his burro, something from my cultural past. The visitor took them."

"We should have discussed it first."

"Perhaps. But I don't regret it."

She passed her scanner over the black hexagon again.

"I'm not getting any readings on what it's made of. But it's not emitting particle or EM radiation, so it's not likely to fry us. Not right away, anyhow. Let's go back." She moved the hexagon into a pouch, and they left the chamber.

LAUREN PICKED UP the black hexagonal artifact from her workbench and inspected it. Its two large sides were flat, one smooth, with a series of circular indentations around the perimeter. She set it down with the smooth side facing up, then touched an indentation. A filigree of strange multicolored symbols played across the shiny black surface.

"Hello," she whispered, her eyes widening.

Pulling out her comm, she entered Ved's secure extension.

"What's up, Lauren?"

"I'll be over in fifteen minutes."

JAN LOOKED UP as Ved marched past her desk toward Magdi's office.

"He's in," she said with an ironic smile as he entered.

Ved knocked on the doorframe and headed to the coffee thermos. He glanced around, then waved a finger and pointed at his ear.

Magdi shook his head. "No bugs today." He came over and refilled his mug. "I know that look," he said, studying Ved.

"You might want something stronger than coffee in that mug. You won't like this."

Magdi closed his eyes. "Tell me something I don't already know."

"OK, executive summary. An intruder has entered the site on three consecutive nights, starting right after staff began setting up the operation. They came in during sleeping hours. These incidents are related to the images shown at our last meeting. We don't think the competition is involved. And we have more evidence." He moved his chair next to Magdi's. "Julio Ortiz installed a cam before the last intrusion." He set down his tablet and scrolled to the images of the visitor and the hexagonal artifact.

Magdi stared at them, alarm on his face. "Any idea of what we're dealing with?"

"None. Lauren's studying that hexagon."

Magdi shook his head, eyes wide in disbelief. "Who are they, and what are they doing?"

"Those are the questions. Lauren's working on it, but she's in the dark, too. We don't know who they are, where they're from, what they're doing, or what they're capable of. Apparently, they were removing something from the black structure. Their behavior pattern indicates they may have finished. Until we know more, we assume our staff and facilities are at risk. This stays under wraps. If the board finds out—"

"It won't be long until every freak and hustler in the system is swarming over us. Whatever, it's just a matter of time before this leaks out, so we need a plan to control the narrative. The last thing we need is Julio's images of the intruder getting out."

Ved nodded. "Picture the news feed headline: *Alien invasion of Sol System underway!!!*"

Magdi closed his eyes and massaged his temples. "Ved, please don't do that."

"We'll deal with it, Magdi, like we always do. Anyhow, Lauren's arranging a move of the artifact and our data to a new facility on Penrose Habitat. She and the crew can work there in isolation, without distraction or attracting attention. This should help the crew avoid accidental information leaks. They understand the situation and are trustworthy, but everyone makes mistakes. The exceptions to this sequestration are Roy Frankhauser and Joe Leighton. They're old hands in the business, and we need them on other projects. Their profiles show the probability of them leaking information is negligible. There could be further intrusions. Julio pointed out that there may be more such structures deeper in the mine. The crew are shutting down operations and mothballing the heavy gear on site. We'll try to collect more data if we can, but we're getting the crew out of there ASAP."

Magdi closed his eyes and leaned back.

"Ved, please tell me this is all a hoax. That site's ore body is one of the best in our inventory."

"What ore body? The site's a dry hole, as our data will soon show."

"When?"

"As soon as Lauren's done scrubbing ... excuse me, processing the data."

Magdi grimaced at the ceiling.

"We should get together soon with her and figure out what to do with Site 1287 if it attracts attention. The competition knows an asteroid of that size can't be worthless, and if somehow it is, it would be seen as a liability. It could be tricky for AZ to explain keeping title to it. And, we can expect the board genius to pull something out of his ass. I've heard he's nosing around asking questions."

"No problem, Magdi. After Lauren's board presentation, Bernie Grant will be licking her boots. As for the expense, remind the board that Alpha's pissed away a lot more on his hare-brained schemes. Lauren and I will figure it out. Just tell them we've reexamined the data. It seems we've found some unfortunate mistakes in the initial assessment of the site's commercial viability. That will buy us time to maneuver."

Magdi nodded, walked to a cabinet, then returned with a bottle of amber liquid and two glasses. He gave Ved a conspiratorial look.

"Dr. Rao, apparently, a low-level technician failed to properly maintain a survey probe. And they've since left AZ for a new position over in Theta Sector. Or was it Iota? Gosh, I just can't recall, but I'm sure Jan can find their file. And it will be a damn shame the tech left no forwarding address."

Ved shrugged. "These things happen, Dr. El-Said."

"Yes, they do." Magdi filled the two cocktail glasses and then handed one to Ved.

"Here's to science." He raised his glass.

Ved clinked his glass against Magdi's.

"And to technology,"

VED WALKED INTO the emergency repair module to find Jeff reclining in his chair with his feet up, staring at displays. Jeff sat up, put his feet on the floor, and looked at Ved.

"How is Magdi reacting?"

"As expected. He's on board with how we're handling things. Any more trouble here?"

"Nope. Everything has been getting done on schedule."

"Excellent. I'm going over to the mine. Inform the crew we'll meet in the office when I get there."

Jeff nodded and opened the mine broadcast channel.

"Attention all staff. Meet in the office in fifteen."

VED NODDED TO each crew member as they entered the office and took their seats.

"Thank you all for handling this business so well. Vice President El-Said and I appreciate your calm professionalism. As you know, starting with the breach, we've kept this site under a communication blackout. You know why; our visitor must remain a secret. Magdi and I have leaked a plausible story. It seems a minor meteorite strike caused the breach, and Lauren and I are here to investigate a rare strategic mineral referred to cryptically as 'Mineral 207-D.'"

"Oh please," Floyd muttered, shaking his head.

Ved looked at Floyd and nodded. "And, incidentally, to collect engineering data after the meteorite strike. We'll tell the AZ board that inconsistent initial survey data triggered a site reevaluation. New data show this site is a dry hole. Beyond that, we're not sure how the Sol System population would react if word gets out about a mysterious intruder at a remote asteroid mine. Rumors would start swirling about a first encounter with an alien culture. You can imagine the rest. So, we're going to manage the information flow, and for the immediate future, that means none. For our purposes, we'll refer to this asteroid simply as 'Site 1287' to avoid mention of the name 2060RT2 after we leave.

"Magdi agrees with our plans to shut down the mine. We'll transport all valuable and portable equipment back to Hawkington and mothball the rest here. Roy will post a detailed schedule on the rec room display. He is arranging your transportation to a lab on Penrose Habitat when the shutdown here is complete. Magdi and I appreciate your willingness to stay and finish this work. You can still choose to evacuate immediately. Just let Lauren know."

Ved looked around at his silent audience.

"You'll keep working according to your contracts, but under Lauren at the new Penrose installation. Your previous confidentiality agreements still apply. Lauren and I will stay to help shutdown the site." He looked around the group. "We're interested in your ideas."

Floyd raised his hand.

"Ved, how restrictive will the Penrose work be?"

"Until we know more about the visitor, you'll remain in that facility. We'll control outgoing comm traffic. Lauren and I believe you're all trustworthy, but people make mistakes. Magdi doesn't want to take any chances. You understand why it's necessary for a while. Lauren will make your stay in the Penrose lab pleasant and productive. Besides her projects, you can continue your education via the University's online catalog."

BHANI, FLOYD, AND Julio sat in the rec room, finishing the beer. The heavy mining equipment had been prepared for on-site storage, and the rest packed for transport back to Hawkington. This included Joe's cam, since no staff would be returning to service it. Joe, Jeff, and Roy had left earlier in the emergency module for Hawkington.

Floyd looked at Julio. "Have Roy or Lauren talked to you about our next project?"

"Lauren mentioned work in the new lab, but no details."

"After this, I'm ready for something nice and sedate," Bhani said. "I'd even settle for boring."

Julio gave her a wry smile.

"For a day or two. Then you'd be climbing the walls. No, I think sedate or boring are unlikely."

That night, there was no intrusion.

THE SHUTTLE LANDED at Hawkington. Lauren carried her duffel and Zubie down the boarding ramp and through the dark, after-hours silence to her office. Senior AZ researchers had access to most databases. For some, alterations required special permission. But Lauren relished challenges to her technical skills and rarely bothered getting formal clearance. She made changes to the inventory database, showing nothing proprietary or important remaining on Asteroid 2060RT2. As long as the Alpha Zubrin Corporation held the asteroid's title, access should be restricted.

Should be.

A slight smile crossed her lips as she recalled one of Floyd's bon mots.

And life should be fair and lunch should be free.

But an asteroid the size of a dwarf planet would certainly attract attention and raise questions. Why would AZ endure liability exposure by keeping the title if it was worthless? Perhaps to use it as a staging area for future work? Or to lock it up, so competitors couldn't use it? Who would believe that?

Her display wallpaper showed a high-resolution image of the abandoned mine complex. In the background, beyond a jagged rock horizon, lay the surreal, star-sprayed infinity of the universe. Wiping a tear from her cheek, she shut off her workstation and looked at Zubie, resting in her lap. She pulled her journal from the duffel and penciled a last entry.

> *It's been hard to stay focused these last few days. At 2060RT2, we saw evidence of intelligence from such a distance that any connection seems miraculous, yet it happened. In a fantasy,*

I run on the asteroid's surface after them, shouting "Please come back. We're here. Come talk with us, if you can." So clearly these things I've seen are not of our Earth. Only in idle daydreams have I imagined such an encounter. Now it's happened. They've come. But who? And for what? It's hard to sleep now. Worries arise over what could go wrong, what I fear will go wrong. I'm frightened and excited. I sense we all will soon face the biggest challenge of our lives. We have to refocus, re-prioritize, and act. I have confidence in Magdi and Ved, in their abilities, their intentions, and their character. I wish I had confidence in my own.

She put Zubie into his travel cage, turned off the desk light, and left the office.

8

BERNIE GRANT STRODE into the dimly lit Hawkington Tap Room and glanced around. Despite the early hour, there were already a half dozen tavern patrons seated at tables and around the bar. At a far corner table, a middle-aged man in an expensive tailored suit sat facing outward. He gazed at Bernie as he approached the man's table.

"Mr. Karpov." Bernie nodded as he took the lone chair facing the man, who stared hard at Bernie.

"Mr. Grant, your payment did not arrive per the terms of our agreement. Need I remind you of what those are?"

"My apologies, Mr. Karpov. My organization's cash flow has recently suffered unexpected—"

"Mr. Grant, the cash flow irregularities of your organization are the concern of neither myself nor my associates. After your last visit to my establishment, you left the consort in such a condition as to require extensive medical treatment. A substantial cash payment was necessary to mollify her parents. When we arranged your reimbursement of this cost, you assured me, and by proxy my associates, that your position on the Alpha Zubrin corporate board secured access to items of a certain liquidity, as you so artfully put it. But you are failing to meet the terms of our agreement. You do understand, Mr. Grant, that you may force us to take the matter to the next level."

Bernie began to perspire.

"Mr. Karpov, please, you must understand—"

"No, Mr. Grant, you must understand. You have one week from this moment to make your payment. If you miss this deadline, you will find yourself newly employed at one of my remote sites, servicing clients whose tastes in amusement are even more exotic than your own."

Karpov glanced at a large man seated by the bar and nodded to him. The man rose from his chair, walked over, and stood behind Bernie.

"Do I make myself clear, Mr. Grant?"

LOGAN AWOKE TO his bedside alarm, showered, shaved, brushed his teeth, and put on a clean jumpsuit. He took the stairs down to where Avala sat at a workstation and looked over her shoulder.

"What's up?"

"Just rearranging information."

"Fascinating." He pointed to the icons and symbols scrolling across the display. "And that is …?"

"Data."

"Gosh, who'd a-thunk it? Please humor my tiny pea brain with an explanation."

"There's an item I need you to get for me."

He leaned back and stretched. "Why am I not surprised?"

"Hush." She waved him off with an amused sideways look.

"The item's in a warehouse. I'll draw you a map and—"

"Hold it. Just what is this item?"

She tapped an icon, and a black hexagonal object sitting on a lab bench appeared on the display.

"So what is it?"

"We'll find out after you get it."

"Oh really? What's my motivation?"

"Trust me, Logy. It will be well worth your time and effort."

"Trust. Nice word, that. So, how do you go about getting this sort of information?"

She waved a finger, and the display went blank.

"Let me give you an example. Firm A's board consists mostly of three types. The first is the virtual sociopath, motivated solely by greed and personal ambition. Next is the ideologue, the true believer, who thinks they've found the one correct way. Third is the facilitator, the glue holding everything together. I work on this last type. Once they're compromised, the first two quickly descend into squabbling, gamesmanship, and general dysfunction. Big egos, turf battles, and internal score settling guarantee mediocre results at best. Competent and productive people are resented, even feared, and they tend to not last long at Firm A. So, a crafty player can go right to work getting into their systems."

"How does Firm A survive?"

"Through political connections and corruption. When they searched for a new communications head, I altered their data so they would hire a certain individual. This person installed the security protocol he developed for his dissertation topic. My analyzer cracked it. Too bad both he and his major professor missed the protocol's flaw. Yet again, a toxic combination of ego, ambition, and self-delusion undermined actual science. But the professor steamrolled the committee, our boy got his degree, and I got access to any system using the protocol, including systems of companies they contact, such as Alpha Zubrin Corporation. AZ would be horrified if they knew this, but we're not going to tell them."

Logan folded his arms and cocked his head.

"How do you know you can trust me?"

She gave him a thoughtful look.

"Because, Logy, if you step out of line, I can blow the whistle on you."

"Really?"

She contemplated the ceiling.

"Let's see. Logan Rhodes, sole employee of New World Consulting, LLC. Background in finance and information technology, now mostly working in private investigations. Thanks to the crooked legal bottom-feeder you hired to handle your divorce and bankruptcy, you were investigated for links to organized crime."

"Wait. I hired him because he was all I could afford. I had no idea he was a mob tool."

She gave him a sly look.

"I know that, Logy, but I could point to more embarrassing lawsuits and possibly illegal improprieties and tax shenanigans. If I didn't know better, I might say you've been a naughty boy." She gazed smugly at him with half-lidded eyes. "I think you get the point."

He fixed her with an incredulous stare.

She smiled and nodded. "Yes. That's right."

"You wouldn't."

She sat like a blue sphinx, arching her eyebrows and smiling serenely.

He glared at her. "Snake."

"Ah-ah." She wagged a blue index finger. "Attitude."

Logan squirmed and flashed Avala a sour look.

Her smile widened. "Gotcha!"

His eyes narrowed. She grinned.

"What? Cat got your tongue?"

He leaned toward her, his glare narrowing. "Just wait for the payback."

Logan gestured to the hydroponics area. "How does this relate to your plans?"

"A hobby. It's fun and a plausible cover story. Plus, I make some credits with consulting projects, and it all looks legit to the nosy. Let's go sit on the terrace."

She rose and looked over her shoulder at him, gesturing for him to follow.

"I was scanning Alpha Zubrin's asteroid inventory for the Pelitat consulting project when I noticed something. I found records of three dry holes, and one of them had suspicious data."

"Wait. What's a dry hole?"

"Before AZ commits resources to an asteroid, they do two bot surveys. If both return good data, more bots install some basic infrastructure. If all goes well, a team visits the complex briefly to finish the setup. After that, the site runs on automation. If the preliminary survey data come back bad, AZ labels the asteroid a 'dry hole', meaning it has no commercial viability, and AZ writes off the initial expenses. They know their business, so dry holes are rare."

"And ...?"

"And here's the thing. One of the three dry hole records contained altered data. You would have to use a complicated statistical analysis to detect that. Whoever did the altering apparently figured no one would. But my routine did the work, and the third dry hole's data are bogus. That third dry hole is an asteroid designated 2060RT2."

"Please tell me you're getting to the point."

She flashed him a distasteful look.

"I checked on the AZ staff who ran that show. In the archive, I found an internal memo that was accidentally routed to an executive named Magdi El-Said. It was apparently unexpected and never read before it got archived." She handed him her tablet.

To: Ved Rao, Hawkington R&D

From: Dwayne Kouba, Projects Lab

Ved, per recent conversation re/ artifact from Site 1287
(see attachment), unable to determine structure or function
with equipment in current facility. Must put project on hold
until relocation to new lab is complete.

—Dwayne

Logan handed the tablet back to her. "And ..."

"And the image you saw earlier, the black hexagonal object, was the attachment to that memo. I think there's a connection between the fishy dry hole designation and this so-called artifact. I looked at the personnel files. Magdi El-Said is Vice-President of Operations. He assigned Lauren Chen, a science staffer, to work with a Dr. Ved Rao, a senior scientist in the research division, for a few days at a location referred to as Site 1287. It's unusual for staff at their levels to work together at remote sites. I found no records of that site or what they did there. Anyhow, Lauren Chen's career at AZ was advancing nicely when she suddenly left the company and started her own firm, Nebula Consulting. It's conveniently close to a new AZ lab going up on Penrose Habitat. Something hinky is going on there, and it might affect Pelitat's access to asteroids in that area.

"None of the lab inventories or archives I've found report this artifact. It looks like there's an effort to keep it hidden. I suspect Dwayne Kouba still has it, but doesn't know what it is. The date stamp on that memo file is very recent. I think it's connected to the 2060RT2 data alteration; apparently, someone wanted no more activity on that asteroid. So, you're going to get this so-called artifact for us."

"Us. Uh-huh. My head's hurting already. Gosh, I wonder why."

"Kouba is moving his work to the new lab on Penrose. He's putting his lab gear into temporary storage in a warehouse near the new lab until the lab setup is complete in a few days. I found a shipping manifest showing the gear going there includes a box of Kouba's personal items. I'll bet we find something interesting in that box. That's where you come in. You're going to retrieve the artifact from the warehouse.

"What makes you so sure it's in the box of his personal items?"

"The staff packing the lab gear inventory every item. Kouba's likely keeping the artifact hidden. That would fit with there being no information on it anywhere, except in the memo he sent to Ved Rao. That slip-up was our ticket in."

"Assuming I agree to this, how do I get it?"

"Simple."

"You've got some kind of nerve using that word—"

She leaned close. "Hush. Like I said, simple. You're Barton Alford, an engineer with Schwarzschild Electronics. You're studying the effects of particle radiation on a microchip embedded in a multimeter used briefly by AZ."

"What?"

"That multimeter is no longer used. It may or may not be listed in any inventories. You'll visit the AZ warehouse with a request to inspect any old units they have in storage. This will get you near Kouba's personal items. Find the artifact and bring it back. What could be simpler?"

"And what could possibly go wrong?" He shook his head, staring at her. "You continue to amaze me. Are you even remotely for real?"

She gave him a satisfied smile.

"I'll drop you at the Ellis transport terminal today. Catch the shuttle to Penrose. You'll stay the night in a hotel and then take a taxi to the warehouse tomorrow morning. When you're done, take the shuttle back to Ellis, and I'll pick you up at the terminal."

She handed him a multimeter, a scanner, and a set of documents verifying his identity as a quality control engineer. She also included an itinerary, notes for his search, and an untraceable credit chip.

9

LAUREN AND VED entered Magdi's office and went to the lounge nook. Magdi stood and shot his cuffs.

"We may have a problem."

Lauren looked at him.

"Site 1287."

"That was quick," Ved said.

Magdi nodded. "2060RT2's closure has been noticed, and word is spreading. We need a solid plan. If it seems AZ has abandoned the site, the competition will go there, if for nothing else, to see why we closed it. I'm sure they're aware of its true value. It may also attract looters, and pirates and organized crime have moved into similar facilities."

Ved looked at Lauren. "What's your take on the intrusions, the black structure in the mine vent chamber, and the hexagonal artifact?"

"Ved, I can't help thinking we may have a first encounter on our hands."

Magdi looked at her with a raised eyebrow. "And that's because …"

"Occam's razor, Magdi. We have an intruder wearing a pressure suit of unknown technology. They appear to be tending an unidentifiable structure in the vent chamber. The purpose of that structure and how it got there are mysteries, and it's made of material we can't identify. We have a hexagonal device with no detectable function other than producing characters not matching any known language. All that's missing here is a green-tentacled, purple bug-eyed monster."

Ved nodded. "As much as I hate to say it, Magdi, I'm inclined to agree with Lauren."

Magdi regarded them for a moment.

"OK. Then we need a plausible reason for AZ hanging onto the asteroid. Ideas?"

Lauren and Ved exchanged looks, and Lauren spoke.

"Research."

LOGAN EXITED THE shuttle on Penrose Habitat and walked to the dorm cubicles serving transient clientele. It was a noisy, multi-storied honeycomb of coffin-size units, but some larger ones at ground level had a desk and a bathroom. Avala had reserved one for him. He showered and then lay on the bed and was soon asleep.

IN THE MORNING, Logan stepped out of the taxi at the AZ warehouse. He was wearing an expensive conservative business suit and carrying a polished leatheroid briefcase. Dark glasses added a dash of casual importance. He walked into the warehouse and approached the receptionist's desk. A haggard, middle-aged woman sat behind it, working a terminal. The display's light reflected off her face as she pecked at the icons. Her ID tag showed her as Sarah Winkler.

Logan removed his dark glasses. "Ah, excuse me, Ms. Winkler, I'm Barton Alford from Schwarzschild Engineering. I believe my office assistant contacted you about my visit."

She looked him up and down, then worked her terminal and inspected a document.

"Very well, Mr. Alford. I'll have someone escort you to the storage facility. Wait here."

She spoke into her headset mic, and a young man in a security uniform appeared.

"Mr. Archibald here will escort you to the storage area."

Logan made eye contact with the guard and followed him down a corridor. They walked through a series of dimly lit storage areas, the sounds of their shoes echoing in the cavernous gray structure. They passed row after row of racks holding white boxes until the guard halted at one of them.

"You should find the item in this area, sir. Buzz me if you need to look in another area."

He handed Logan a pager, then turned and headed back toward the office.

Logan rummaged through the boxes on the first shelf and found nothing. He climbed a short ladder to the next shelf and repeated the procedure. Glancing around, he saw no sign of the guard. He stepped down to the floor and pressed the pager. Soon, the clacking of boots announced the guard's approach.

"Thank you for coming, Mr. Archibald. I don't seem to be able to locate the H56B unit. Perhaps it was misplaced, maybe with Dr. Kouba's personal gear."

The guard scrolled through his tablet's display.

"That's over in D section." He led Logan to another area. "It should be about here, sir." He stood and watched as Logan inspected the contents of several boxes.

Then Logan saw it lying at the bottom of a box, a black hexagon. At first glance, it appeared to be random lab junk. Turning away from the guard, he pulled the multimeter from under his jacket.

"Ah." Logan held it up. "Here it is." The guard flashed him a bored look. Logan opened his briefcase and pulled out the scanner. "Damn. Battery's nearly dead, and I need to scan this unit. You wouldn't by chance have an extra Type-B power cell lying around, would you? I just need it for a minute."

"I'll see if I can find one, sir."

Logan watched him disappear down the corridor. He slipped the hexagonal artifact into a dark cloth bag and put it in his briefcase. The guard returned with a battery, and Logan inserted it into the scanner. He pretended to scan the multimeter, then left it in the storage box. He turned to the guard and handed him the battery.

"All done here. I have all the information I need. Thank you so much for your help, Mr. Archibald."

The guard nodded and then headed back toward the office. Logan followed, detouring into the washroom, where he took the artifact from his briefcase and slipped it into a shielded vest beneath his shirt. Even through the cloth bag, the vest, and his T-shirt, it felt cold against his body.

Back at the front desk, Ms. Winkler nodded at Logan, her face blank.

"Did you find what you needed, Mr. Alford?"

"Yes, Ms. Winkler. And thank you for your help."

She pointed at the scanning gate. "We'll need you to step through that gate, please."

A drop of sweat trickled down Logan's back as he walked through the scanner. No alarm sounded, and he maintained a steady pace toward the exit.

LOGAN PAUSED OUTSIDE the door, then looked around and put on his hat and dark glasses. Glancing at the auto-taxi dock, he saw an array of security cams. One was aimed at the door he had just exited through.

ShitShitShit

He looked down and walked briskly around the warehouse. In the alley, he continued toward the Penrose Habitat shuttle station. Soon he heard the sounds of a slowing vehicle followed by doors slamming and the rapid shuffling of feet over pavement. Logan turned into the wooded strip beyond the alley and began a halting run through the thicket. Behind him, he heard a shout and the thrashing of feet overtaking him through the undergrowth. He tripped, stumbled forward, and dropped his briefcase.

Logan wheeled around and a man drove his fist into what would have been Logan's solar plexus. Instead, his fist slammed into the artifact with a cracking noise. He shouted in painful surprise, then staggered back, clutching his injured hand with the other. Logan stepped forward and drove the base of his right palm up against the man's nose, snapping his head backward. Blood erupted from his nose and mouth. Stepping into him again, Logan jerked his right knee into the man's groin, then snapped his left elbow into the man's jaw. Logan's attacker collapsed into a groaning heap. Logan went through the man's pockets and found a stun gun. Its charge level was 100%. He crouched and moved through the wooded strip, away from another man searching the alley.

Logan went roughly a hundred meters through the wooded strip. Seeing no pursuers in the alley, he moved back onto the pavement. He walked rapidly until he saw a man in a dark suit enter the alley ahead and look around. Before the man saw him, Logan crouched behind a trash bin and waited. As the man came past the trash bin, Logan raised the stun gun, and when the man looked in Logan's direction, he pulled the trigger. The man's pockets yielded another stun gun, fully charged, which Logan slipped into his briefcase. He retreated to the wooded strip and moved on.

LOGAN EMERGED FROM the wooded strip behind an office building next to the shuttle terminal. He peered around a corner and saw two men in dark suits standing a few meters from the boarding tube, watching the foot traffic. Logan withdrew into the wooded strip and texted Avala:

Marsh goons watching shuttle area—can't return yet.

He went through the wooded strip to the dorm cubicles and spotted a vacant unit in the rear. Inside, he stripped and took a shower, then lay on the bed. His comm buzzed, and he read the message.

Are you OK?

Yes. Barely. Will attempt return when goons are gone.

OK. Worried.

Don't be. Have seen worse.

OK.

Logan used the shuttle app on his comm to check the schedule. The next one stopping at Ellis would leave in two hours. He set a timer, closed his eyes, concentrated on breathing, and dozed.

LOGAN'S COMM BUZZED, and he awoke. He dressed, put on the hat and dark glasses, and went to his observation spot near the transport area. It was late in the evening, and the goons were gone. He used the shuttle app to pay his fare for the trip to Ellis, then moved briskly through the boarding area. He flashed his comm past the boarding scanner as he entered the tube along with several other passengers. Inside the shuttle, he took a seat and examined the hull cam display. The only people outside were ordinary passengers. The shuttle got underway, and Logan breathed a sigh of relief. He texted Avala:

Boarded shuttle. En route to Ellis.

THE AIR TAXI deposited Logan on the lab's helipad, and Avala met him at the entrance, concern on her face. She watched in wide-eyed silence as he removed his jacket, then withdrew the artifact from under his shirt and handed it to her. He looked at her.

"What? Cat got your tongue?"

"Logan, I was so worried—"

"About that?" He pointed to the artifact. "Yeah, well, have fun with your new toy."

Her green eyes were wide with anxiety. "Logan, are you angry with me?"

He closed his eyes and rubbed his face.

"No. I'm still wound up. Things got ugly and I hurt two men. They may have deserved it, but I feel lousy about it."

Logan walked to the refrigerator and retrieved two bottles of beer. He handed her one and went out to the balcony. She followed, and they sipped beer in silence and gazed into the dark.

LOGAN WAS READING his tablet when Avala appeared.

"Interesting developments."

He folded his arms and looked at her. "And?"

"Are you up for a trip?"

"Dare I bother to ask where and why?"

"Remember that dry hole I told you about? Asteroid 2060RT2? That's where. The why is I want to inspect the complex."

Alarm registered on his face, and he set down his tablet. "Please, tell me you're kidding."

"We leave in fifteen. I advise showering before we go."

"Wait, are you saying I need a shower?"

"We won't have time or facilities during the trip. Now git."

He shrugged and headed up to his apartment.

THIRTY MINUTES LATER, Avala landed her two-seat helicopter at the Ellis space terminal. She and Logan walked down a long corridor past hatches leading to docked craft. She stopped at one and pointed.

"This is it."

"This is what?"

"Big Snake. Cobra Mark Ten. We board through here." She worked a door pad, and they followed a dimly lit ramp to another hatch. She entered the lock code and then the hatch opened, and they stepped into the ship's cockpit.

"Grab the seat on the right."

Avala secured the hatch. Logan eased into the copilot's seat and fastened the straps as Avala worked the console switches. The cabin lights and ventilation came on, and she gave him a thumbs-up. To the rear, he saw a kitchenette, a bunk, a lavatory, and hatches.

"You'll want to get comfy," she said. "It's a long ride."

"Like how long?"

"Several hours, depending on circumstances. There's a foldout bunk back there and an entertainment console with movies, music, and games. Or I have some interesting drugs."

"What kinds?"

"Mostly hallucinogens and soporifics. No stimulants."

"What? No stimulants?"

"Logy, I really hope I don't have to explain that to you."

"If you did, I probably wouldn't get it anyhow. So, what hallucinogens?"

"Let's see." She rummaged through a clear plastic bag of multicolored capsules and pills. "Your pick of silly, confusing, or profound."

"I'll go with the soporific."

Avala handed him a large red capsule.

"Drinks and snacks are in the fridge. Use the bunk straps. See you in the next century, space cadet."

Logan took the capsule and retreated to the bunk. Putting on a headset, he inspected the music menu and chose Russian violinist Viktoria Mullova playing Bach's "Partita Number Two" in D minor.

LOGAN OPENED HIS eyes in darkness. He heard only the faint sound of the ventilation system and the soft murmur of Avala's voice. He unbuckled the bunk straps, then sat up and looked into the cockpit. Flashing console icons threw a pulsing glow onto her face as she worked the controls and spoke into a headset. Despite the calm precision of her voice and motions, she radiated tension through the sheen of her damp skin.

"Ship, scan that rig again, and reopen the sector hailing frequency."

The neutral female voice of the Cobra's AI replied.

"Commander, the vessel is not responding on sector hailing frequency."

"Ship, deploy and arm all hard points, and enter primary evasive pattern."

"Acknowledged, Commander."

"Logan! Get up here and strap in!"

He sat in the copilot's seat and buckled the harness. "What the hell is going on?"

"Commander, hard points deployed and armed. Now entering primary evasive pattern."

The Cobra went into a series of sickening twists and accelerations.

Avala worked the control console.

"Ship, open wide-spectrum hail."

"Wide-spectrum now open, Commander, and I have scan results."

Logan watched a stream of incandescent projectiles fly past the Cobra on his display, some hitting the hull with loud thumps. He looked at Avala and could see the muscles working around her jaw.

"So, you want to play rough, do you? Ship, bring us into attack pattern, and report scan results."

"Commander, scan shows an unidentified Sidewinder-class pursuit ship."

Gripping his seat, Logan looked at Avala, and she flashed him an evil grin.

"Ship, designate the Sidewinder as target one and switch to manual controls."

She seized the flight sticks and glanced at Logan.

"I told you this would be fun, Logy."

"You and I clearly have different definitions of fun."

He tightened his harness and watched the display. Avala guided the Cobra through a series of maneuvers, and they moved directly behind the Sidewinder.

"Ship, set radar weapons lock on target one."

The Cobra tailed the Sidewinder precisely.

A few minutes later, the Sidewinder stopped maneuvering and settled into a straight course at a constant speed. Avala looked at Logan.

"I think they got the point."

"Commander, we are being hailed on the sector frequency."

A frantic voice crackled through the cockpit speakers.

"Hey, please don't shoot! I screwed up. I'm sorry!"

She adjusted her headset mic.

"You shot at us. Why? And who are you?"

"My name is Robbie Tucker. I work for a security contractor named Burwell Solutions. I just started this job last week. My first assignment was to find a bad guy. I thought you were him. My mistake."

Avala looked at Logan and shook her head.

"Alright, Robbie. Hold your course."

"Will do. Just don't shoot."

She turned to her console, then tapped a series of icons and inspected the display.

"So, Robbie, I got Burwell's data, and it looks like you're telling the truth. We'll let you go now, but you need to school yourself on ship ID procedures. Keep the sector hailing frequency active and don't be so trigger-happy. Send over your credentials, because you're paying for my hull repair."

"Roger that, Cobra, and thank you."

The Sidewinder's engine flared to life, and the vessel moved off.

Avala shook her head. "Kid's lucky I'm in a good mood."

Logan let out a long breath. "I hope I don't find out what happens when you're in a bad one."

THE AI GUIDED the Cobra as Avala operated a data console, and Logan gazed at the vastness of space on the copilot's display. A navigation icon flashed, and the ship AI came on the cabin speaker.

"Commander, the scanner is picking up a surface structure on 2060RT2."

"Bingo!" Avala grinned at Logan. "A dry hole wouldn't have surface structures."

He watched the display as the Cobra slowed in its approach to the facility. A network of tracks on the asteroid's surface led to large doors built into a rock wall. The Cobra's landing gear deployed, and the craft settled onto the asteroid's surface.

"Ship, maintain position until we return."

"Acknowledged. Commander, step with caution. The surface is slippery, and gravity is low."

"The power system should still be viable."

Logan caught her eye. "How would Alpha Zubrin react to us being here?"

"They wouldn't like it one bit, but they won't find out, so just relax and enjoy things."

"Whatever you say, Commander."

"That doesn't sound very relaxed."

They suited up and headed to the complex entrance.

Avala studied the front hatch, then spoke through her suit comm.

"Interesting. This numerical pad unlocks the hatch manual controls. It's disabled, and the hatch is unlocked." She worked the controls and slid the hatch open. "The office is to the right and the mine to the left."

They stepped into the tubular corridor, and Avala slid the

hatch closed. She opened the office airlock's first hatch, and they entered the vestibule. The hatch closed behind them. Repeating the process, they stepped into the darkened administrative unit.

"Hopefully, power's still available," she said.

"What if it's not?"

Ignoring Logan's question, Avala approached a console and consulted her tablet. In the narrow beam of his flashlight, Logan gazed around the interior at desks, terminals, lockers, odds and ends left behind, and more doorways. Avala worked a bank of switches, and the lights came on.

"Sweet!" She looked at him. "Now for atmosphere and heat. We should keep our suits on. The cleaning bots and air scrubber will take a while to clear the dust. And we'll need to rinse our suits in the Cobra's airlock before we board."

She busied herself at the console while Logan looked around the unit. Soon a string telltale showed air flowing through a ventilation grid.

"We're getting atmosphere," she said. "Watch that wall monitor to your left. Water will be available after the system thaws."

"Are we planning to stay?"

"No, but it would be nice to know everything works. If it does, we could come back."

"Sure. This would make a great vacation spot. If the Ellis jail is full."

The display showed a steady increase in air temperature and pressure. A few minutes later, the readings were in the comfort range.

"Hey," he said, "air looks good now."

She inspected the console. "We've got normal gas composition.

Let's see how to deploy the cleaning bots." She worked the system control interface, and two small machines emerged from lockers near the floor. They began moving, their appendages wielding several cleaning attachments.

"Those bots will take a while. Let's go back to the airlock and check the decontamination system."

When they returned, she consulted her tablet and operated the office console.

"The data system is up. Interesting, there's a document here. Someone forgot to delete it. Probably in a hurry to leave."

Logan looked over her shoulder.

"I would be. Talk about claustrophobia. I can't imagine living here."

He walked to a small stateroom. It contained a closet, a chest of drawers, a tiny washroom, and a bunk next to a window. In a corner sat a small, shallow box holding a granular material. In the closet were sheets and covers for the bunk, all neatly folded. The view out the window showed the tubular corridor connecting the office to the mine and dark, rocky hills in the distance.

"See anything interesting?" Avala asked from the office.

"Not yet. Let's check out the rest of the complex."

"I got this document open. Come here and look."

He walked over as the file's contents appeared on the display.

NOTICE:

ASTEROID 2060RT2 AND ALL SITE CONTENTS ARE
THE PROPERTY OF ALPHA ZUBRIN CORPORATION.
UNAUTHORIZED VISITORS ARE ADVISED TO LEAVE
IMMEDIATELY OR BE HELD IN VIOLATION OF APPLICABLE
TRESPASSING LAWS.

Now that I have your attention, and you are no doubt quaking in fear of our legal department, a few words before you go. Anyone who has gotten as far as you have is likely aware of the nonsense in AZ's site evaluation report. We had good reason to evacuate this facility. I urge you to leave now and forget about this place. But I doubt you will, so I ask that your subsequent actions be informed by compassion for other living beings.

L. Chen
Operations Scientific Director

Avala nodded as she looked at the display. "So, Lauren Chen was here."

"And that's one interesting message, especially the closing sentence."

"I agree. Let's take that little stroll." She jumped up, hit the ceiling with the flat of her left hand, and landed on the deck, grinning.

Logan recorded images as they walked around the site. Coming to the other side of the office unit, they walked past the tube corridor. Avala pointed to the elliptical seam around the repaired breach.

"Look at this."

"That looks like a repair patch."

She leaned close to the tube.

"If it's a patch, it seems unlikely it would appear identical to the surrounding material. See the fine surface irregularities at the ellipse's edge? They match perfectly to corresponding irregularities in the patch. That needs explaining."

"Maybe the elliptical section was removed and then reattached. But why would they do that?"

AVALA AND LOGAN went around the office and through the front entrance hatch. Facing the mine complex airlock, she worked its interfaces, and they stepped into the main corridor of the crew quarters. Walking through the hallway, they looked into each room as they passed.

"Another reason this can't be a dry hole," Logan said, "is it was an active operation. AZ sank a lot of resources into this. They had one hell of a good reason for leaving."

"I agree. Let's figure out what it was."

He looked at her, and she pointed, then kept walking.

"I haven't seen any security cams," he said, "have you?"

"No. I guess the staff didn't think they needed any."

He followed, and they continued down into the mine, past machinery that was parked and covered. Other than footprints and machine tracks in the dust, they saw no indications of any living creatures, human or otherwise.

Then they found it. They stood and passed their flashlight beams over the black structure in the vent chamber.

Logan whistled. "Wow. This must be why Chen was here. Any idea what it is?"

Avala scanned the black structure, took images with her cam, then stood staring at it.

"There's something vaguely familiar about this material, but I can't place it."

She climbed onto the big rock and took more images.

"Logan, look at this."

He stood on the rock and looked down at the open, empty cells.

"Those holes are hexagonal, the same shape as the artifact. I'm thinking," he said in a conspiratorial tone and giving her a sly look while tapping his helmet, "there's a connection!"

She gazed up at him with a smirk. "You think?"

"I've been known to do so on rare occasions."

She smiled at him. "Ready to go?"

They walked back toward the mine entrance. Along the way, Logan switched on the lights in the crew quarters. Folded bedding lay neatly on the bunks, and clothes lockers stood open and empty. He shined his flashlight around the corners of the rooms.

"They didn't leave much behind."

"Let's investigate the crew and what happened here. I suspect Dr. Lauren Chen has answers to many of our questions."

THEY CLEARED THE Cobra's airlock, took off their suits, and then strapped into their seats. Avala tapped a console icon.

"Ship, take us back to Ellis Habitat."

As the Cobra lifted off the asteroid, Logan reclined his seat, his eyes glued to the copilot's display.

A minute later, the ship AI spoke.

"Commander, we have been scanned. I detect a Viper-class vessel at approximately ten kilometers and closing rapidly."

10

AVALA SAT UP. "Ship, put hailing channel on cabin speaker," she said as she ran a series of console commands.

"Cobra, eject your cargo, or I will destroy you."

Logan looked at her and gripped his seat. The AI came over the speaker.

"Commander, do you care to respond?"

"Negative. Ship, deploy and arm hard points and begin primary evasive pattern."

As she operated the control console, something struck the Cobra with a loud bang, sending vibrations through the hull.

"Ship, switch to manual controls and give damage report." Avala gripped the control sticks, and the Cobra swung wildly through a series of nausea-inducing maneuvers.

"Commander, hard points deployed and armed. We have taken minor damage to the left rear hull, but no breaches."

Avala gripped the control sticks.

"Ship, weapon designations: primary ballistic cannon, secondary heavy laser."

On the cockpit displays, glowing projectiles swarmed past the Cobra as Avala flew it through a series of tight spiraling turns.

Logan watched as part of the attacker's ship appeared on the left edge of his display. A moment later, the entire vessel was visible and moving closer to the display's center. They were getting on its tail. He looked at Avala. Her skin was deep blue, and her eyes were wide, unblinking black pools.

"Ship, reset weapon designations: primary heavy laser, secondary ballistic cannon, tertiary light laser."

"Acknowledged, Commander."

"And now, Big Snake eats little snake."

She opened up on the Viper at a range of two hundred meters. Logan watched as laser and projectile strikes tore chunks from the attacker's hull. A port opened, and an object sped away from the vessel.

"Commander, missile launch detected. Commencing countermeasures." Logan heard the sounds of machinery ejecting chaff. "Anti-missile torpedoes deployed." A green light flashed on the console. "Missile attack neutralized. Opponent has taken significant damage and is losing maneuverability."

Avala's muscles tensed visibly beneath her now-purple skin.

"Ship, set comm to broad spectrum hailing. Viper, cut your engines and stand by or be destroyed."

There was no reply. The Viper tried to jink out of the Cobra's line of fire. Avala worked the control sticks, and laser strikes appeared along the Viper's hull. More debris came off, and soon the target was drifting and rotating slowly as vapor plumes leaked from many spots on its damaged hull.

"Commander, target has zero effective acceleration vector and inactive engines. How do you wish to proceed?"

"Lock all weapons on the Viper and maintain range one hundred meters."

The Cobra adjusted speed and followed the vessel, which began leaking vapor from several more points on its hull. Logan gripped his seat and stared at the spectacle unfolding on his display.

"Ship, track any objects leaving the target."

Logan looked at Avala. Her skin had returned to a lighter blue, and her eyes were glittering emeralds. She gave him a sly smile.

"What should we do with him, Logy?"

"Well, those missiles made me think he was seriously trying to kill us."

She nodded and pressed a button. He watched the display as a burst of projectiles slammed into the Viper's hull, and it erupted in bright flashes and flying debris. A pair of coffin-sized pods shot from the Viper's side ports just before the ship exploded in a blinding flash. Logan cringed as chunks of the Viper banged off the Cobra's hull.

"Ship, designate those pods as targets one and two. Follow target one at fifty meters and track target two for later retrieval."

"Acknowledged, Commander."

"What are we doing?" Logan asked.

She glanced at him with an evil smile. "We'll get target two later."

"What's the plan for target one?"

She worked the controls, and the Cobra soon overtook the first escape pod. She pressed a button, and a bright flash appeared on the pod's rear, followed by debris and a vapor plume as the pod spun off in a new trajectory.

"Ship, deploy cargo scoop and retrieve target two. When target two is secure, activate cargo bay life support. Put the cargo bay cam on display A."

"Are you just going to leave target one like that?"

She gave him a sideways glance. "What, are you my conscience now?"

"Do I need to be? They could just be an innocent hostage."

She gazed at him for a moment.

"Ship, transmit target one's current velocity vector to nearest law enforcement. Advise immediate rescue, and pod occupant should be held on suspicion of attempted piracy."

"Acknowledged, Commander."

Logan watched the display as the Cobra moved over target two with a faint clunk. The AI spoke.

"Commander, target two is secure in the cargo bay. Now activating cargo bay life support."

Avala turned and looked at him. "Watch the display to your right."

The cargo bay interior appeared, showing the pod grappled to the center of the floor.

"Ship, alert me when anything emerges from target two."

"What should we do with him? Assuming it's a him," Logan said.

"Well, the extreme options are we let him go ... or we kill him."

He frowned and shook his head.

"Not my choices, either, Logy. At least not the first one."

"Then we hand him off or we keep him."

"I'd rather keep a rabid hyena."

"We should hand him off to law enforcement."

"The nearest agencies are Sector Security and Ellis Health and Safety."

"OK. Sector Security."

She shook her head.

"Totally negatory. One, they're corrupt, and two, we can't let them find out about us."

"So that leaves the local police."

"Unless you can think of something else."

The comm speaker bleeped. "Commander, the occupant of target two has emerged."

AVALA AND LOGAN looked at their displays. A wiry man in a stained gray jumpsuit stood braced against the pod, casting a cautious look around the cargo bay. Avala straightened up and leaned forward.

"Ship, run an ID scan on the cargo bay occupant." She turned to Logan. "Let's see who we have."

"Commander, public data have yielded a tentative facial recognition. The occupant appears to be a wanted fugitive named Daniel Larkin."

"What information about him can you get?"

"Obtaining detailed list of offenses from public data," the AI said. "Larkin is wanted in several sectors for armed robbery, hijacking, piracy, smuggling, extortion, attempted rape, and indecent exposure."

Logan looked at Avala. "Indecent exposure?"

She held her index finger to her lips, winked, and switched on the comm.

"Mr. Larkin."

The man's head jerked with alarm, and he looked around the cargo bay.

"Mr. Larkin, you attacked my ship. Would you care to explain why?"

He braced himself against the pod, his feet hooked under the grapples as he looked around wildly.

"You got the wrong guy! I'm not Larkin! I'm just hired help."

Avala shut her eyes. "Mr. Larkin, wasting my time will not improve your situation. Go look into the scanner by the hatch."

He crossed his arms and stood motionless, staring at the hatch. Avala rolled her eyes and toggled her mic switch.

"Ship, reduce cargo hold air temperature to zero Celsius." She winked at Logan and toggled her mic. "Mr. Larkin, you can adjust the cargo hold air temperature at the wall interface after you confirm your identity. Otherwise, it's going to drop to ambient, outside the ship."

She sat back and flashed Logan a smug grin.

Larkin freed his feet from the grapples and kicked over to the optical scanner. A few moments later, a message appeared showing a positive ID. Avala inspected the display.

"Mr. Larkin, you've been a very busy boy. And a very naughty one."

Larkin cleared his throat. "What are you going to do?"

"Oh ... I dunno. Maybe we'll get back to you, maybe not. Byeeee."

She toggled the sound off, and the displays showed Larkin yelling or screaming. She gave Logan a look of satisfaction and then shut off the displays.

"We need to sort this out now. We can't keep him in the cargo bay much longer, and I'm not taking him back to the lab."

Logan nodded. "So it's Ellis Health and Safety then. Who can we arrange a handoff with?"

"I don't know yet."

"Do you think he has any connection to Marsh?"

"I doubt it. Marsh would be scraping the bottom of the barrel to hire someone as low as Larkin. He wouldn't be able to handle anything they needed done. He's just a random pirate. Our bad luck."

He raised an index finger. "Get the Health and Safety employee roster. It should be in public data."

She worked her console, and a minute later, Logan's display showed the Ellis H&S personnel list.

He scrolled through the roster.

"Forget about administrative staff. Support staff, no. Ah, here we are, field staff. So, I'm thinking, we need to find someone who would have a reason to cooperate without trying to screw us or blow our cover. How about here? Look, I've got the staff listed by hire date, most recent first. The newer ones are less likely to be corrupt and more eager to score points with a bust like Larkin."

She nodded and gave him a thumbs-up.

"Here we go," he said. "Aram Terzakian, recently hired and probably still on probation. Collaring Larkin would be good for his rating. And his last employer was—"

"Zandax Security, now owned by Marsh. Well done, Logy. Let's find out why he left."

He looked at the data. "Terzakian probably wasn't enough of an asshole to suit Marsh."

Avala laughed as she worked her console.

"Wow. Marsh still has the same IT bozos, and they still haven't figured out Zandax's system. We could have some real fun here."

"First things first. Why did Terzakian leave?"

She worked her console, then sat back and stretched.

"It seems Marsh fired our Mr. Terzakian for insubordination."

Logan nodded. "I was right. Not enough of an asshole. Any info on what that was about?"

Avala frowned and shook her head.

"No details. Some up line suit pulled the plug on Mr. T. I think he's our man."

"Agreed. Now, to make contact."

"I'll send him a quick hello with Larkin's CV attached. That'll get his attention."

BERNIE GRANT STRODE into the new AZ laboratory on Penrose Habitat and paused in the reception area. The room contained a few easy chairs facing a wall display, but was otherwise empty. Opposite the entrance, a young woman sat behind a glass window. She looked up at him and smiled.

"Good morning, sir. How may I help you?"

"I'm Bernard Grant with the Alpha Zubrin Corporation Board of Directors. I'm here on board business to see Bhanupriya Oka."

She gave him a puzzled look. "One moment, please, sir." She tapped her headset mic and turned away for a minute, her voice inaudible.

"Sir, Ms. Oka is currently unavailable. I will be happy to pass along your message."

She pushed a pad of paper and a pencil through a slot below the window. Bernie glared at her and ignored the paper and pencil. He walked to the door by the window and rattled its handle. It was locked.

"I demand to see her! I'm on important business, and I don't like having my time wasted."

The receptionist turned and spoke into her headset. A minute later, Lauren came through the door, closed it, and leaned against it with folded arms.

"Mr. Grant, this facility houses proprietary research operations. It's closed to the public. If you have a message for Bhanupriya Oka, our receptionist will pass it along."

"I am not the public. I represent the Alpha Zubrin Cor—"

"My receptionist told me, Mr. Grant."

"Then you know I'm here on important business."

"I'm not up to speed on board doings, Mr. Grant. Why do you want to see Bhani?"

"That's none of your business."

"Mr. Grant, I'm Bhani's supervisor, and it is very much my business. Please put your message to her in writing, and I'll see that she gets it."

Bernie stared at Lauren as beads of perspiration swelled on his reddening face. She went back through the door, and it locked behind her with a solid clack.

TERZAKIAN SAT AT a terminal in the barracks day room. He was looking over his duty schedule when his pocket comm vibrated. A new message appeared with an attachment.

This may interest you.

He linked his comm to the terminal, then checked the auto-scan output. The link protocol made the message untraceable. He opened the attachment and sat up as he read Larkin's rap sheet and the list of outstanding warrants. Terzakian stepped to the kitchenette, poured a cup of coffee, and thought for a few minutes. He went to the terminal and hit "reply."

You have my attention.

He watched the screen.

You want him?

He typed a reply.

What's the deal?

The deal is we hand him off to you.

In exchange for what?

You take him off our hands in three hours. We stay anonymous.

Three hours is a no-go. Too soon.

In three hours we airlock him.

I'll see what I can do. Give me thirty minutes. What do I call you?

Kokab

Terzakian checked his watch and worked his pocket comm for a few minutes. Then he typed another message on the terminal.

Kokab: Handoff at Zebra Station.
It may take me an hour to line it up. See you there.
A. Terzakian

The reply came seconds later.

OK.

AVALA INSPECTED THE Cobra's flight system console, then the hull cam display.

"Ship, get data on Zebra Station."

"Commander, Zebra Station is a small trading depot one hundred and fifty-three kilometers from Ellis Habitat. It is a privately held business. Current owner-operators include three generations of the Russell family. It rated four out of five in terms of amenities. It is within the regular patrol radius of Delta Sector Security, and it has no history of criminal activity."

TERZAKIAN'S UNIT HUMMED.

Heading for Zebra. Be there, or we space him.

Very well. I have plans for him.

I'll bet you do.

IN THE H&S lounge, Terzakian looked at Hana.

"Larkin is wanted by System Central on inter-sector charges. Is Central going to give us any grief for nabbing him, us being mere habitat health and safety?"

She shook her head. "Let it try. Central has no authority over sectors. It needs reminding that it works for the confederation, not the other way around. Delta Sector could burn Larkin at the stake tomorrow if it decided to. So, how bad is he?"

"Larkin isn't the worst the sector has to offer. He's just a crook. It's the ideologues I'd worry about. I'd rather deal with a crook—crooks just want your money."

AVALA SHUT OFF her comm, slipped it into a pocket, and gave Logan a thumbs-up.

"We're going to get rid of this turkey and score some local points. Ship, head for Zebra Station. Idle there at five kilometers and scan for fighters in the vicinity."

"Acknowledged, Commander."

THE COBRA IDLED five kilometers from Zebra Station. There was no traffic. Logan and Avala inspected the well-lit structure on their displays, which showed a landing port on the station's apparent underside.

Avala poked an icon on her console. "Ship, switch to station-hailing frequency."

"Done, Commander."

"Zebra Station, this is Cobra mark ten Foxtrot Tango Whiskey seven zero niner requesting docking permission."

The cabin speaker crackled.

"Cobra," a male voice said, "this is Zebra station. You are cleared for docking on the primary port."

"Ship, approach the landing zone, and hold ten meters above the pad."

"Acknowledged, Commander."

The Cobra moved under the station and rotated, so the pad appeared below them. Avala thumbed her pocket comm.

TERZAKIAN'S COMM HUMMED.

> We're coming in, hard points out.
> Don't make us use them.
> Docking with cargo hatch facing access tube.
> Connect and take your boy.
> Careful, he may be armed.
> Try not to shoot up our cargo bay.
> We'll be in touch.

Very well, Kokab.
—T.

AVALA DOCKED THE Cobra in a rotating descent. Logan's display showed arrays of multicolored lights, antennae, and deck hardware. People watched through observation ports as the Cobra settled onto the pad at Zebra Station.

"Ship, set drive to idle and cargo hatch to auto deploy."

"Acknowledged, Commander."

She refreshed the display showing the cargo bay, but left the audio off. Larkin was gripping the pod and staring at the hatch. A faint clunk sounded and the access tube latched onto the Cobra. The cargo hatch opened into the access tube's interior, and two figures appeared in the entrance, holding onto support grips. One wielded a sidearm pointed at Larkin.

There was a verbal exchange, then Larkin took off his flight suit. He was wearing a sweat suit underneath. Following a tense discussion, he stripped to his boxer shorts and then turned and hooked his feet under the pod grapples. He placed his hands behind his back, and the two figures entered the bay. One held his weapon on Larkin as the other snapped wrist ties on him and then took his clothes. They pulled him out of the cargo bay, and the hatch closed with a clunk, signaling the access tube's disengagement.

Avala stretched and looked at Logan.

"Ship, take us home."

11

AVALA AND LOGAN docked the Cobra on Ellis Habitat, then returned to her lab in the helicopter. They were exhausted.

Logan rubbed his face. "I don't know about you, but I'm starved."

She closed her eyes and nodded.

"Right. Dining room in thirty minutes." She turned and went to her quarters.

Logan shuffled upstairs and took a shower. He came back down fifteen minutes later to find Avala sitting at a table with two bottles of beer, condensation droplets sliding down their sides. He grabbed one and took a drink.

"Any ideas about that artifact?"

She shook her head. "Not yet. I need more time."

He inspected her and smiled. She gave him a curious look.

"What?"

"Your mods."

"Do you like them?"

"They're pretty extreme, but yeah, I do. Why did you get them?"

She fidgeted with her comm and stood.

"I should—"

"Ah-ah-ah." He wagged an index finger at her. "You're not going anywhere until I get answers." He pointed at her chair. "Sit. And keep talking."

Flashing him an annoyed look, she flopped back into her chair and folded her arms with a sigh. She shifted her eyes at him, then blew out a long, exasperated breath and shook her head.

"Alright, you should know this anyhow, so it might as well be now. I do some work for Pelitat. They move around, never staying in any one sector for very long. They're involved in things like genetic engineering projects and pelagic habitat design. Their clients prefer discretion and mobility."

"Pelitat sounds like a shady outfit. Are they involved in anything illegal?"

"That depends on the jurisdiction. Pelitat prefers keeping a low profile." She watched him, a curious expression on her face. "My current relationship with Pelitat is as an independent contractor. Before that, I was Pelitat's legal property."

He sat up, his eyes wide. "You were what?"

"You heard right, Logy. Property, as in, they more or less owned me, until I bought them out."

"I thought slavery was illegal. How did you get into that situation?"

Logan watched in fascination as Avala sipped her beer and then ran her purple tongue over her lips, her emerald eyes fixing him with an unreadable gaze.

"It wasn't actual slavery, more like indentured servitude. I was born in a lab in one of their pelagic habitats. One that's not in any sector directory, so don't bother looking."

"How did your parents figure into this?"

"Mommy and Daddy were lab dishes, also the property of the Pelitat Corporation." She gave him a look of wry amusement. "Well, I guess now I really have your attention. Executive summary: Sol System culture would call me genetically engineered, and please stop staring at me like that."

"Sorry. So, your personal mods aren't really mods?"

"Correctamundo."

"Well, Avala, I think you look terrific, if I may say so."

She smiled. "You may, Logy."

"Back up. You said Sol System culture. Relative to what?"

"Pelitat is not from Sol System. Logan, I'm not from your star system."

"You're having me on again."

"No."

"If you are, Avala, I'll get you."

She gazed at him with a neutral expression.

"Logan, you asked for it."

"What?"

"The truth. If you don't believe me, that's understandable. It's a lot to absorb."

His perplexed gaze narrowed, and he nodded.

"OK. So what's next?"

"We just keep searching for information, avoid becoming a target, and have some fun."

"And how's that supposed to work?"

"There are things I need help with, and I trust you."

"Seriously? That's not the impression I got from our last discussion of trust."

"From what I've seen of you, Logan, you're thoughtful and

compassionate. I saw how you tried to look after the skin jobs when you believed they were human children, and how you reacted when I destroyed them. You felt remorse over hurting those men on Penrose. How you reacted when Larkin tried to jack us, and I almost abandoned that disabled escape pod. You're self-reliant, no stranger to hard work, have some sense of ethics, and you're not afraid to speak your mind."

"A regular boy scout."

She shrugged. "Touché. Plus, I like your sense of humor, you're fun to have around, and you are kind of cute. These are traits I value in a companion. And because, Logy, I have the goods on you. And you know it."

"That you do. But trust is a two-way street. How do I know I can trust you?"

"I'm hardly in a position to hurt you, needing you as I do. You'll have to take a chance with me." Her luminous emerald eyes locked on his. "Can you do that, Logan? Do you think you can trust me?"

"Right now, I don't even trust myself. I think I'm in an exhaustion-induced waking dream."

LOGAN FOUND AVALA on the atrium balcony, hunched over a tablet and munching from a bowl. He sat the table.

"What's the plan?"

"No plan yet. Pelitat wants the artifact but won't say why. I figure you and I have first dibs on examining it, so let's focus on getting information. That includes how Lauren Chen and the mine crew are involved. Maybe you can snoop on the crew. I'll be in the data room."

Avala strode off across the atrium, and Logan watched her slender frame move and sway in her sheer, tightly wound sarong. Overhead, the tree creatures browsed, occasionally tossing berries down to him. He used his tablet to search for information on the mine crew, but came up with nothing. He shut off the tablet and headed for the data room.

Finding the artifact on a table by Avala's console, Logan inspected its black, shiny top surface.

"Any idea what that is yet?"

She looked up at him and shook her head.

"No. I've got icons coming up on its surface, but nothing I can make sense of yet. Hopefully, Chen made some progress with it. Question is, where are her data? We may need some help here."

"From who? We can't let anyone know we have this thing, can we?"

"Not just anyone."

"Who then?"

"Rapunzel."

Logan gave her a puzzled look. "Who is that?"

"My assistant."

He looked around. "I haven't seen anyone else here. Where is she?"

She gave him an impish look and pointed to her console.

"Right now, in there. Rapunzel has an instance in this system."

"What does this Rapunzel do?"

"Some data gathering and analysis. Whatever I don't have time for. She handles incoming contacts and plays games with nuisance callers until they go away. Ask her about the amusing conversations she's had with unauthorized callers."

"What if it's important?"

"They give Rapunzel a code phrase, and she talks with them."

"Alright then. Show me how this algorithm works."

A tone sounded, and an indignant female voice came over the wall speaker.

"Logan, I do not appreciate being referred to as an algorithm."

He gave Avala a wry look. "Not bad."

She winked at him and held up an index finger.

"Rapunzel, disable argumentative mode."

"Very droll, Avala, and at any rate, not advised."

"Rapunzel, I've changed my mind. Disregard that last request."

Logan looked at her. "Request? Exactly who's in charge here?"

Avala ignored the question.

"I need to go see what Chen stored in AZ's Hawkington archive. You should go, too."

He frowned at her. "So, we just show up and hope nobody recognizes us?"

She rolled her eyes and huffed in exasperation through her pursed lips.

"Please tell me you're being deliberately dense. What do you think of Rapunzel?"

He cupped his hands on the sides of his mouth.

"Rapunzel's not bad, for an algorithm!"

"I heard that, Logan."

"OK, Rapunzel, are you a who or are you a what?"

"That's for me to know and for you to find out, Logan."

Avala turned from her console. "Rapunzel, please come here."

A young woman strode in from an adjoining room and stood looking at Avala.

"Rapunzel, meet Logan."

He shifted in his seat and gave her a wary look. She was of average height and wearing a tight-fitting gray jumpsuit over her trim, athletic frame. Her smooth, unlined face was of indeterminate race. Her gold-tinged skin and confident, straight posture radiated robust health. She had large, calm gray eyes, high cheekbones, and a straight but unremarkable nose. She was wearing her light-brown hair brushed into a knot on the back of her head, held in place by several flat-black pins.

Rapunzel held out her hand. "Good to meet you, Logan."

Avala observed them with amusement.

Logan reached out and shook Rapunzel's hand, then threw an irritated look at both women.

"Synthetic intelligence, my ass. You two were having me on. Enjoying yourselves?"

Avala simpered.

"Ooh, I do believe I detect a note of skepticism. Rapunzel, please educate Logan on your abilities."

Rapunzel turned to him.

"Logan, imagine a mix of genetically engineered biology, nanotech, electronics, and mechanical systems."

"I assume you're also from Pelitat. Why haven't I seen you before now?"

"I've been busy in my office." She pointed to the adjoining room's door.

"All the time I've been here? Didn't you get bored, restless, curious?"

"Until my work is done, I designate those things as irrelevant."

"Then you've got more self-control than I do."

She gave him a sideways look and arched an eyebrow.

"Correct, Logan."

He gave her a crooked smile.

"I see you have Avala's sense of humility. Are you two by chance related?"

Rapunzel gestured toward the wall, and a display lit up. She pointed at a table.

"Avala, sit here with your hands on the tabletop. I'll show my connection with the system. Logan, tell me what you'd like to see on that display."

He thought for a second.

"Show the schematic for the optical disk reader at the Hawkington Library."

Rapunzel folded her arms and gazed at the display. The schematic appeared, complete with the device's name and library reference number.

Logan nodded. "Alright, let's try another one. Rapunzel, project the image of a chimpanzee sitting on a Bactrian camel."

The image immediately appeared on the display.

"Not bad. One more. Rapunzel, project your image with no clothes on."

Avala snorted and rolled her eyes. "Oh, puh-leeze."

Giving Logan a wry look, Rapunzel snapped her fingers, and her nude image appeared on the display. Logan grinned at her.

"Very nice, Rapunzel, I'm impressed."

"With what?"

Avala gave him a look.

"Rapunzel, I guess I owe you an apology," he said.

Avala snaked an index finger to the console, and the image vanished.

"I need to finish some things here. I'll see you two in the atrium later."

LOGAN TOOK THE stairs up to his apartment and went out onto the balcony. He braced his palms against the railing, closed his eyes, and tried to focus on his breathing as the elfin tree creatures flocked down to greet him.

This can't possibly be real. I must be losing it.

A moment later, the tiny gnome-like animals grew quiet, casting curious eyes at something behind him. He turned and saw Rapunzel standing in the doorway.

"Does Avala need me?" he asked.

"No. I'm just curious." She looked out at the light rain falling on the forest. "Do you have time to talk?"

"Sure. What about?"

"I don't know. I want to learn."

"Anything in particular?"

"About Sol System, its people, and you."

Rapunzel's placid gaze was steady, her gray eyes clear and unblinking.

He leaned back against the railing and gave her an appraising look.

"The system connection you displayed was very impressive. Is it always on?"

"No, just when I choose it to be."

"So, the rest of the time …"

"I'm like you and Avala, mostly."

"Is that primarily how you see yourself?"

"More like entirely how I see myself. How do you see me?"

"That seems to change by the minute. Right now, I see you as smart, capable, and interesting."

He pointed at the tree creatures on the railing, eyeing her with fascination.

"I think they agree. At least on that last point."

A slight blush passed briefly across her cheeks, and she looked away.

"You're not comfortable with compliments," he said.

"I find them indistinguishable from flattery, which I understand to be manipulative."

"Are you speaking from experience?"

"Yes."

"Where?"

"Pelitat."

"People there tried to manipulate you?"

"Of course. Standard procedure. So please forgive my skepticism."

"Healthy skepticism is always in order."

"You approve?"

"Does it matter?"

"Yes, it does."

"You need approval?"

She looked out at the forest. "Not so much need as want."

"Do you need anything?"

"Responsibility and purpose."

"Both can be a burden. Certainly the first. I don't know about the second. What about companionship and love? Do you have any awareness of those?"

She looked puzzled for a moment. "I'm not sure. Aren't they the same?"

"I'm not sure either. What are you sure of?"

"So far? That reality in Sol System is not exactly deterministic."

He laughed. "I wouldn't put it so politely; it's practically random. Is there anything that you are sure of?"

"That I'm driven to explore, but I sense limits, and I'm trying to reconcile these thoughts."

"There's something worse than sensing limits."

"What?"

He looked out at the evening rain. "Never finding them."

She gazed at him for a moment, then redirected her attention to the dark mist beyond the railing.

"My awareness and emotions are growing."

"That's a normal development in Sol System culture. Your biggest asset will be a sense of humor."

She gave him a slight smile. "I've gathered that. What else is important here?"

"Understanding why people search for meaning in their lives. Many find it through a purpose. Have you experienced that?"

"I think so. I started as a companion and assistant to Avala. But that may be changing."

"Into what?"

She shook her head, her eyes fixed on the forest. "I'm not sure."

Logan looked into the dark expanse beyond the balcony.

"I once considered having a purpose. But it implies some kind of grand plan, and I never saw one that made any sense."

"Logan, I think you have a purpose."

"Oh? What?"

"First, to endure."

"Sometimes that seems like the biggest challenge of all. What comes after that?"

"What do you see?"

"I don't know. So much has happened lately. I have to reevaluate everything I've taken for granted."

She gazed at him for a moment. "I feel I have a better understanding of you now, Logan."

"Likewise. I'm glad you're here, Rapunzel. You're excellent company. And quite interesting, for an algorithm." He gave her a wink.

She gave him a mock frown. "As Avala would say, I'll get you for that."

He grinned, backed away from the railing, and stretched.

"And I look forward to it. Now, if you'll excuse me, I need to take a shower and change clothes."

"I've enjoyed talking with you, Logan."

"So, you can enjoy things."

She gave him a thoughtful look.

"Enjoy. That's a word I've heard Avala use often. Many at Pelitat consider it irrelevant. I'm coming to an understanding of it, and I like it." She turned and left the balcony.

LOGAN ATE BREAKFAST in the atrium and took his coffee to the terminal room. He found Rapunzel working a console.

"Where's Avala?"

She looked up and smiled.

"Avala will be here shortly. There's someone here now you should meet. You'll be working with her on the next project." She turned in her chair, then folded her arms and looked at him, a smile playing at the corners of her lips.

"Project? Who?"

She tapped a console icon, swiveled her chair to face the door, and pointed. A slow clacking of shoes in the corridor grew louder until a plump middle-aged woman in a wrinkled, worn business suit entered the room. She had an unruly mass of flaming-red hair, pale freckled skin, blue eyes, and bright red lipstick.

Rapunzel observed Logan and the woman.

"Good morning, Dr. Kuznetsova," Rapunzel said.

She waved absently at Rapunzel and then sat down heavily in a chair, fanning herself.

"Whoosh! Those stairs. I must catch my breath."

Logan looked at Kuznetsova and then at Rapunzel and gave her a suspicious frown.

"Logan, this is Dr. Elena Kuznetsova, head of research at the Alpha Zubrin facility on Sagan Habitat."

"Nice to meet you, Dr. Kuznetsova." He smiled and shook her hand.

Kuznetsova and Rapunzel exchanged looks and then burst out laughing. Kuznetsova winked at Logan with an unmistakable smirk.

He squinted at her. "Kuznetsova my ass! That's one hell of a disguise. OK, what's going on here?"

"Well, Logy boy, Dr. Kuznetsova is going to get us, or rather me, into the Alpha Zubrin archive. Only bona fide AZ staff can access their offline databases. Archive staff are unaware that the real Dr. Kuznetsova is attending a family reunion in another hab. So, in she goes. It'll take a couple of hours to get what I need. You'll have time there to explore."

LOGAN AND AVALA walked down the shuttle boarding tube into the Hawkington transport terminal. They stopped and inspected the large street map posted near the exit.

"Let's meet outside the Hawkington Taproom in two hours," Avala said. "Have fun." She shuffled off into the underground complex.

Logan strolled through the labyrinth of stores, shops, and small businesses, making his way up into the surface domes. These original structures had restricted access now that the underground complex was complete. He got a thirty-minute pass and then wandered through the domed areas, enjoying the view of the city and the Martian landscape. In the Hawkington Taproom, he ate a sandwich, then left.

LOGAN FOUND AVALA sitting at the end of a bench, reading her tablet. She had set her bag so that no one could sit close to her. She glanced at him and then kept reading.

"How did it go?" she asked in a low voice, staring at her tablet.

He took out his tablet and tapped the interface. "I gave myself a nice tour and had a snack. You?"

"Rapunzel coached me on the accent. The archive staff didn't ask for my ID. That's too bad; she did a great job on it. Let's take a walk. Pretend I'm your grandmother and help me up." She hooked her arm through Logan's for support, and they walked in a slow shuffle.

"The records on Asteroid 2060RT2 were scrubbed," she said, "and there's nothing useful about it left in this archive. Lauren Chen is definitely involved, and I think she moved some data. I found internal memos and reports coincident with the bogus survey data. Magdi El-Said assigned her as a temporary mine science officer. I found no mention of why, where, or for how long. It's unusual for someone at her level to be assigned to an on-site position like that. I found reference to a 'Site 1287', but its connection to anything is unclear. Rapunzel is looking into that and any involvement of Chen's immediate up line, Dr. Ved Rao."

They strolled along the walkway, glancing casually at the shops and business fronts.

"I noticed something else. Besides Chen, two other AZ scientists have recently left Hawkington, and the new secure lab on Penrose hab is complete. Nebula Consulting just updated its sector security record. Guess many staff it lists?"

"Three."

"Correctamundo, Logy, Chen and her two colleagues, including Kouba. It's not clear yet why they left AZ and created this firm, but I suspect someone was in a hurry to get them off Mars."

"Why?"

"To avoid scrutiny, I think. The four mining staff assigned to 2060RT2 have also left—"

She stiffened and gripped his arm.

"Don't look up. Don't look around. Keep walking smoothly."

He kept a steady pace and looked straight ahead.

"What's going on?"

"That office front we just passed ..."

"Yeah?"

"It had security cams at the top of the outside wall."

"And?"

"The building logo was for Marsh Systems."

"Oh, shit."

"Yes."

Her grip on his arm tightened.

"Turn left at the next corner. When we're away from the cams, we move faster."

THE TECH SAT drinking coffee and glancing between a wall display and a tablet. A console beeped, followed by a flashing red display light and the message:

Alert: Positive Fugitive ID

The tech read the details, adjusted his headset mic, then punched a console button.

"Reed, Jackson, we got a match. Check comm images and get out there, pronto. We need them for interrogation."

As Logan and Avala walked down the alley, the sound of marching feet behind them grew louder.

"We're being followed," she said. "Take the next right. Keep walking. Don't look back."

As they turned the corner, she released his arm and then disappeared behind a ventilation node.

12

JOE LEIGHTON STOOD in the entrance of the posh AZ executive dining room. In a far corner, he saw a large man sitting alone at a table. He saw Joe and then beckoned him over.

"Bernie Grant," he said, extending his hand.

Joe shook his hand.

"Joe Leighton. Thanks for inviting me to lunch, Mr. Grant, but I'm curious about why."

Bernie forced a rigid smile. "Please, Joe, call me Bernie."

Joe took the opposite chair. "Alright, Bernie."

Bernie cocked his head and scrutinized Joe.

"I understand you were on the mining staff at 2060RT2 when it was an active operation."

Joe regarded him for a moment.

"I was sent there on a repair team. The site was shut down before any active operation."

"What did you repair?"

"Didn't you see the report? I thought board members had access to that sort of thing."

The server walked over and stood by their table. "Would you gentlemen care to order lunch?"

"Yes," Bernie said, "and put it on my account."

Joe grinned at the server. "What do you recommend, my man?"

"The Deluxe Executive Club Sandwich, sir."

"I'll have two. And a serving of chocolate mousse cake, a banana split, and an IPA."

"Very good, sir! And I assume you'll also be having the soup and salad?"

"Absolutely, but just one of each."

The server turned to Bernie. "And you, sir?"

"I'll have the club sandwich. Just one." He gave Joe a critical look.

The server departed, and Bernie focused his hairy-eyeball stare on Joe's placid gaze.

The IPA arrived, and Joe took a sip. "Damn, that is one tasty brew. Thanks, Bernie!"

"What did you have to repair?" Bernie asked with a bogus smile forced through clenched teeth.

Joe set down his ale and wiped his lips. He shrugged and smiled blandly.

"A hole. In an external corridor. Caused by a meteorite."

"If there was no valuable ore, that operation would just waste resources. Why did El-Said do that?"

"That's also in the report, Bernie." Joe reached for his ale.

Their food arrived, and Joe dug in as Bernie stared at him.

"What kind of communication was available to Chen and Rao?"

"Same as the rest of us," Joe said between bites. "Standard extranet plus some secure links. Why?"

Bernie's complexion shifted from florid to a moist, sallow pink.

"Did Chen and Rao communicate with El-Said while they were at the site?"

Joe put down his sandwich.

"I'm unclear, Bernie, on where this is going. Can you spell it out for me?"

Bernie's hairy-eyeball expanded as Joe watched, stifling a smirk with a sip of ale.

"I need evidence of El-Said's plan to sell equipment from the site to our competition, starting with a list of the equipment left there."

Joe sat back with raised eyebrows and shook his head.

"I know nothing about that. I returned to Hawkington before the site was shut down. You'll need to read the report and the inventory." Joe reached for his sandwich.

Bernie glared at Joe as he finished the last bite of his first sandwich, then pulled over the chocolate mousse cake. The big man stood, threw down his napkin, then stalked toward the door. Joe looked up.

"Thanks for lunch, Bernie!"

Joe caught the attention of the server, idly rearranging silverware on the next table. The server came over, and Joe pointed to his second sandwich.

"Can I get a bag for that, please?"

The server grinned at Joe. "Absolutely, sir."

Joe reached for his banana split.

THE SOUND OF footsteps behind Logan in the alley grew louder, and he broke into a sprint. He headed to the next intersection in the maze and turned right. Spotting a pile of building materials near a trash bin, he seized a two-foot piece of composite pipe and crouched behind the bin. A moment later, the sound of stamping feet paused, and Logan heard heavy breathing. He watched a shadow advance past the bin, a weapon extended forward. When the man appeared, Logan swung the pipe down onto his weapon arm. The man bellowed, dropping a pistol onto the pavement and cursing. Logan threw down the pipe and bolted from behind the bin.

"Stop or you're dead, asshole!" another voice shouted from close behind.

Logan turned and saw a pistol bore centimeters from his nose. The first man, gripping his injured forearm, glanced at the one holding the pistol. "Shoot him!"

The second man took a deep breath, then stepped back one meter and adjusted his aim.

Logan heard two snaps, and both men collapsed onto the pavement. Avala emerged from behind a stack of crates, shoving a stun gun into her jacket. With speed and grace incongruous with her appearance, she bounded over and began dragging a man behind the trash bin. She pointed to the other one.

"Pull him over here. Hurry."

Once they got the unconscious men behind the bin, she began stripping them.

"Take everything."

"Shouldn't we at least leave them their tighty-whiteys?"

She snagged the waistband of each man's shorts, then looked inside and smirked. "Yeah, leave the shorts. Put their clothes behind the shrubs. I'll get some bags." She jumped up, dashed out of the alley, then resumed Kuznetsova's tedious waddling. Logan heaped the items behind a bush and then leaned casually against a wall. He crossed his arms and looked around.

A short while later, Avala returned with two bags, one containing items she had purchased to appear like a normal shopper. They shoved the men's possessions into the other bag and left the alley. He held the bags with one hand and her arm with the other as she shuffled along, humming a mindless tune.

After a few blocks, they entered an alley, and Avala looked at Logan.

"We need to move fast." She took off in a trot, the padding of her suit jostling and her handbag bouncing. They continued through a maze of narrow alleys back to the transport terminal. The departure schedule showed forty minutes until the next Ellis shuttle. She pointed to a dorm pod complex.

"We won't be noticed there."

Avala scanned a payment card at the nearest vacant unit's lock, and they collapsed onto the bed, breathing hard.

"That was close," she said. "Keep an eye on the time."

"I'll make the shuttle reservations." Logan entered the payment data at the wall-mounted terminal.

Avala removed the Kuznetsova disguise layer by layer, then stepped into the shower. The naked, athletic blue figure that emerged toweling herself off bore no resemblance to Dr. Elena Kuznetsova.

"Your turn, Logy, unless you want to smell like a horse going back to Ellis."

He looked up at her. "I kind of like the way horses smell."

"Now that I think of it, that's the wrong animal." She flopped down on the bed and closed her eyes.

When Logan got out of the shower, she was wearing gray

sweats and running shoes. She pointed to a set of green sweats on the bed.

"Those should fit, but you'll have to wear the same shoes."

"Great. I'll look like a major dork. You think that won't attract any notice?"

"Trust me, Logy, they won't be looking at you."

At the mirror, she smeared pale cream on her face and hands, covering her blue skin. She put on pink lipstick and a pair of large sunglasses with pink sequined frames. Pulling the hood over her head, she zipped up the sweat top. Like the rest of the suit, it was a revealingly tight fit. Cracking the pod door open, she motioned to him, and they stepped outside.

A YOUNG SECURITY guard stood at the attendant's podium by the loading tube. He looked at them and smiled, his eyes drawn to Avala's figure.

"Good afternoon."

"Hello there," she said. "Are we on time for the Ellis run?"

He stared at her chest. "Yes, and seats are available. ID, please." He pointed to the scanner.

She fished in the pockets of her tight top, twisting to either side to give the guard a thorough view.

Avala smiled at the guard, her dimples drawing attention to her lush, pink lips.

"Ya know, you look just like someone I used ta know."

"Lucky him."

"Yeah, he was lucky." She lifted her sunglasses and winked at him. "Ya been at this station long?"

"A few weeks. This is my usual shift. I get off in fifteen minutes."
He raised his eyebrows and gave her a significant look.

"Thank you, officer." She took Logan's arm, and they walked up the boarding tube.

The guard stared at her backside until another passenger waiting at the podium made a rude noise.

Inside the shuttle, they made their way to the rear. Avala sat and removed her sunglasses, then leaned back in her seat and closed her eyes. Logan flopped into the seat next to her and crossed his arms.

"Was it really necessary to chat up that clown? Marsh is watching for me, and we were exposed. But perhaps you were having too much fun to notice that Captain Square Jaw back there could have detained us."

"Oh, please. Lose the melodrama. He was harmless."

Logan squirmed in his seat, frowning. "Well, I'm just saying—"

She narrowed her eyes at him.

"I was just having him on a bit." She studied Logan and her frown dissolved.

"Oh, wait …" Her simper spread into a wide grin. "You're actually jealous!"

He flashed her a peevish glance. "Strange way to have fun when we're trying to avoid attention."

"And now you're the judge of avoiding attention. Anything else I've done that needs correcting, say, in the last ten minutes?"

He gave her a sullen look. "Clearly, I'm not qualified to correct your behavior."

She looked him up and down. "And yet, somehow, I don't think that's going to stop you."

"I could start right now, if you like."

"I'd prefer if you didn't."

She crossed her arms and stared out the window.

LOGAN SAT ON the balcony of his apartment, splitting his attention between a tablet and the forest. Hearing a knock, he looked up to see Rapunzel standing in the doorway. He smiled at her.

"Hi, come on in."

She walked over and stood looking down at him.

"I'm experiencing unfamiliar thoughts, confusing ones that raise questions I'm not able to answer. I thought you might understand some of them."

He set down the tablet and gestured to a chair. "What are they?"

"Senses of disappointment, frustration, inadequacy, and failure. These are new to me; I recognize them only from their definitions. They are unsettling."

"You're having normal human emotions. Have Avala or I done anything to hurt your feelings?"

A puzzled look crossed her face. She gazed out at the forest.

"I don't know. I'm not sure what that means. It doesn't seem logical. It doesn't make sense."

"For me, wanting to make sense of things is frequent and sometimes debilitating. You're having feelings and looking for things to make sense. That's perfectly normal for people in my culture. Congratulations, I think."

She turned back to him. "Why do you say that?"

"Feelings can cause emotional pain, something you might be

experiencing. If it's caused by something Avala or I have said or done, you must say so. I've spent too much of my life alone, and I can be self-absorbed and inconsiderate. You're one of my few friends, Rapunzel, and I don't want to hurt your feelings. And I'm sure Avala doesn't."

She looked at him for a moment.

"I think I understand, Logan. It must be part of my emergent behavior, which will naturally be affected by my companions, whatever their culture. But I doubt that you or Avala caused it. Why have you been alone?"

"I move constantly to make a living. As soon as I make friends, I have to leave them, and then time, distance, and circumstances erase the friendship. I accept solitude as inevitable."

"That seems undesirable, Logan. Do you have a family?"

He looked out at the forest. "Not in the conventional sense. I never knew my father, and my mother died when I was young. I was married, but that fell apart."

"Why did your marriage fail?"

"We had different ideas of what marriage should be. I saw it as a refuge; she saw it as an arena. Since then, I've kept to myself. Do you have others you feel close to?"

"I feel close to Avala. And to you."

"Thank you for saying that. I'm glad we're friends, Rapunzel."

Her comm buzzed. "Avala needs me in the lab. Will you go with me?"

"Sure. Let's go see what she's up to."

RAPUNZEL AND LOGAN walked into the data room to find Avala

staring at the black, hexagonal artifact and drumming her fingers on the tabletop. Logan sat next to her.

"Any progress?"

"No. Pelitat may have answers. Rapunzel, I'll need your help during the trip."

Logan gave Avala a shocked look.

"What? And leave me alone here, unsupervised? What if I break something or get lost?"

She gave him a wry look. "By now, Logy, you should be able to change your own diapers. Rapunzel, we should get rolling. We'll fly the Cobra and take turns sleeping on the way. Logan, we should be back tomorrow. Try not to burn the place down."

LOGAN AWOKE, SHOWERED, and dressed. Downstairs in the atrium, he ate breakfast and drank coffee. Except for the distant humming of machinery, the lab complex was silent. Walking toward the data room, he glanced out at the forest, now shrouded in a heavy mist. It collected on the glass atrium wall, forming rivulets of water that streamed down in no apparent pattern. On his way, he stopped at the corridor leading to the apartments occupied by Avala and Rapunzel. He paused at the open doors and looked in. Both apartments, like his, were in the style of hotel suites. The furniture was sparse but adequate, bearing a few personal items, and the rooms were immaculately clean.

Except for a few blue and red indicator lamps, the data room was dark. As Logan entered, the overhead lights came on. He checked the comm terminal for messages; there were none. He checked the terminal in Rapunzel's work room; the screen was locked. Logan found nothing that would shed more light on his two companions. He returned to the atrium, refilled his coffee cup, and then went out onto the balcony to enjoy the quiet and read.

LOGAN WAS ON the balcony feeding treats to the tree creatures when a sky taxi settled onto the helipad. Avala and Rapunzel stepped out and walked into the atrium, and Logan came in to greet them.

"Ah, the intrepid travelers return. How did things go?"

Avala gave him a thumbs-up and grinned. "Our Pelitat colleagues were quite helpful. You'll see."

She pointed to the data room and gestured for him to follow. Logan sat at the table while Avala worked her console. The display refreshed with two images of a planet taken from close orbit.

"Those are from the hexagonal artifact," she said, pointing to the display. "Look at the left one."

A terrestrial world like Earth appeared. It had a sky with patchy white clouds, landmasses of varied shades of greens, browns, and purples, and vast expanses of blue ocean. To the right appeared a variety of structures surrounded by agricultural areas. Roads connected the structures with people and animals dotting the landscape. Although the resolutions did not allow clear views of them, the people looked humanoid.

"There are many similarities between this planet and Earth. Consider the probability of evolution producing humanoids on similar planets. It's a statistical certainty that there are many planets in the galaxy like Earth. Here is your first direct evidence." She worked her console, and the left image changed. It showed the same planetary curvature and a similar backdrop of stars. "This is the same planet."

The image showed evidence of advanced civilization. There were dome-like structures connected by tubular links, but the landscape was mostly stark and barren, like a desert. Vegetation was scarce, and the small seas were more brownish-green.

"That requires explanation," Logan said, "but it would probably be over my head."

"It's straight-forward, Logan. Our home world's star changed, and the planet gradually overheated, becoming uninhabitable. The Pelagic people did not cause that. Earth's culture is fortunate. Human behavior changed, reversing your global heating in time to prevent catastrophe. The Pelagic people were not so lucky."

Avala refreshed the left image. "Again, the planet, same orbital perspective."

The atmosphere and oceans were gone, and the world was now barren and lifeless. To the right scrolled images near ground level. They showed ruins too degraded to identify, apparently the remnants of an extinct civilization.

Logan shook his head. "Now that's just depressing."

"Yes, but look." Avala refreshed the screen.

Except for the stellar backdrop, the image could have been from Delta Sector. As far as the eye could see, various ships swarmed about habitats and stations of all shapes and sizes. They were not in orbit around a planet.

"This is the Pelagic culture, our people."

Logan stared at her. "Do they all look like you or Rapunzel?"

"No. We're polymorphic. Genetic and biological engineering

have been routine for many generations. We have various physical forms that are quite distinct. Pelitat's scientists have observed the Sol System culture for a considerable length of time, and your phenotype is quite popular."

"You mean you can choose what you look like?"

"Not entirely. Your culture team makes some initial choices for you, but you can customize later to your heart's content."

"What else did you discover about that hexagonal object?"

"A junior researcher left it on asteroid 2060RT2," Avala said. "She doesn't work for Pelitat directly, so I've never met her. Her supervision says she's conducting research on the asteroid, and there are more sensitive things deeper in the mine. She's worried about what might happen to them; some of them are living creatures. Her supervision wants the artifact returned, but Rapunzel and I talked them into letting us study it a while longer. You've seen some of the artifact's information, and no evidence of violence or warfare on the Pelagic home world. This is notable, considering convergent evolution."

"How?"

"Like your hominids, our ancestors evolved initially through a predator-prey dynamic. Our civilization's peace and prosperity have endured for immense periods of time, an accomplishment of our cultural institutions and bio-engineering. We believe the Sol System Confederation can achieve this as well. The visitor to Asteroid 2060RT2 has left you a message of hope."

"Pelagic scientists could help you remove atavistic violence from your genome," Rapunzel said, "like they did for our people."

"But you kept the knowledge, means, and will to defend yourselves against predators. Avala showed that in dealing with Larkin."

"A collaboration with the Sol System culture is an opportunity the Pelagic people can't afford to pass up. We can start at the asteroid mine. Alpha Zubrin scientists are aware of something happening there. We could initiate collaboration using the mine and the artifact in joint research and development with Alpha Zubrin. We'll need help from your authorities to set this up."

Logan frowned. "We could face some big problems."

Avala looked at him. "Such as?"

"The media, corporations, politicians, the military, organized crime, cultural extremists, lunatics. Any of these could be problematic."

"I see your point, although I think it's pessimistic. Like Rapunzel, I think it's worth the risk. Our Mr. T, Terzakian, may be able to help. Ellis Health and Safety handles law enforcement and security in this part of the sector. The asteroid will be in this jurisdiction for a while. We may need that help in securing the asteroid mine. I sense that Mr. T has connections and is trustworthy. We should see him about this now. What do you think?"

Logan shrugged. "Your call, boss lady."

"I hereby resign from said position of boss lady. This can't be just my decision."

"OK, I'm willing to share the blame. What about you, Rapunzel?"

"Sure. If it doesn't work out, Avala can always fire us."

Avala gave her a narrow look.

"You two are a riot. OK, let's go meet with Terzakian. I'm sure he'll love getting dragged into this."

"Avala, you should probably go in disguise for now," Rapunzel said. "I suspect the Ellis staff could do without an exotic distraction at this point."

"I was looking forward to seeing their reaction to the real you," Logan said, giving Avala a wink.

She tapped a console icon, and the display went dark. "We'll save that bit of fun for later."

HANA SWIVELED HER chair and stood as the trio entered her office at Ellis Health and Safety.

"I'm Hana Ramirez." She shook their hands. "Grab a seat." She pointed to the empty chairs. "Terzakian gave me a heads-up, but no details on what you need."

"Thank you for taking the time to meet with us, Ms. Ramirez," Rapunzel said, handing her a data stick. "We're confident you'll find enough here to make a case." She nodded toward a wall display.

"Make a case?" Hana gave her a curious look, then plugged the data stick into her desk console. "Terzakian should be here any minute. Let's wait for him before we look at this." She leaned back in her chair and studied them with calm, penetrating eyes.

Avala, wearing a wig, brown makeup, and brown contact lenses, looked like an ordinary Sol System resident. "We need your advice and help with something important."

Hana nodded. "I've gathered that—"

Footsteps in the corridor grew louder and Terzakian entered the office.

"Sorry I'm late. I'm Aram Terzakian." They shook hands and then he took a chair.

Hana looked at Avala. "OK. It's showtime. Let's see what you've got." She worked her console, and the display came on.

AFTER THE PRESENTATION, they discussed the images from the mine, the black structure in the vent chamber, and the hexagonal artifact.

Hana looked at Logan. "Did you show this to anyone else?"

"No, not yet."

"This has to go to the Sol System Scientific Council," Terzakian said.

Hana nodded. "How can we help?"

"We need advice on presenting this to the council," Logan said.

"And we have to do it soon," Avala said. "There are likely to be complications."

Hana looked at her. "Such as …?"

Avala turned to Rapunzel. "Tell Hana what you've discovered."

"I've been monitoring comm traffic. Lately, some has involved the coordinates of Asteroid 2060RT2, which is currently AZ's property. I have identified people who might remove, damage, or destroy objects in the mine, and possibly destroy the entire facility."

"Some people value profit over science and living things," Avala said.

"We need to convince the council to prevent looting and destruction at the mine," Logan said.

"What you've shown here is impressive," Terzakian said, "but do you have any physical evidence besides what's on the asteroid?"

Rapunzel nodded. "We have the hexagonal artifact."

Hana and Terzakian exchanged glances. Avala caught Hana's eye.

"We have to prevent unauthorized travel to the asteroid. We hope you and Terzakian can help. The asteroid's currently in Delta

Sector near Ellis Habitat, so it is—"

"In our jurisdiction," Terzakian said. "Chief, can we enforce an access restriction on this asteroid?"

"If the sector governor grants it." Hana looked at the others with a conspiratorial smile. "Are you up for a trip to Hawkington tomorrow?"

"Absolutely!" Avala said, unable to suppress a grin.

"It's up to us to pitch this to the governor," Logan said.

"We'll argue the site has important scientific and archaeological aspects," Rapunzel said, "and it needs immediate formal protection until the Scientific Council has evaluated our plan."

Hana studied them for a moment. "What, exactly, is your plan?"

Logan and Rapunzel looked at Avala.

"We'll propose a study of the hexagonal artifact and the black structure in the mine vent chamber. We'll include a systematic search for more objects on the asteroid."

"Rapunzel's comm monitoring shows that protection is needed as soon as possible," Logan said.

Terzakian looked at Hana. "Well, Chief, what do you think?"

"That this might be fun, but I'll settle for interesting."

13

THE GROUP, HEADED by Hana and Terzakian in their smart dress uniforms, looked impressive as they marched over the plush carpeting. Their destination was the governor's office in the Delta Sector administrative complex in Hawkington.

Hana caught Terzakian's eye, then looked down at their uniforms.

"We don't want the governor to think we're trying to intimidate her."

"Good point. Let's bring up the rear. Avala, you go ahead. You'll make a better first impression than a couple of uniformed goons. Chief and I don't want to scare anybody."

"You two are kinda scary."

Logan glanced at Hana and Terzakian.

"That could actually be a plus. We'll need all the gravitas we can muster for this. Try not to look so easygoing."

Outside the governor's office, the group sat and watched the wall clock tick away the seconds. A minute before their appointment, the office door opened, and a smiling young man in a business suit strode out.

"Hello. I'm Jax Williams, Governor Kayembe's administrative

assistant. She'll see you now." He held the door open for the group, then sat at a desk near the governor.

Governor Kayembe looked up from her work and smiled.

"My assistant gave me a summary of the reason for your visit. Please elaborate." She folded her hands on her desktop and gazed at the group.

AFTER THE PRESENTATION, Governor Kayembe stared at the display for a moment.

"If you do, in fact, have what you say you have, then I'm confident the Scientific Council will give you an audience. But it's not clear to me just what my role is here."

"Madam Governor," Hana said, "we ask that you grant Asteroid 2060RT2 coverage under the Archaeological Sites Protection Act. There are indications the site may be in jeopardy."

Kayembe inspected Hana and then nodded. "I'll have my staff look into it."

"Madam Governor, this is urgent. We have good reason to believe the site may be subject to looting or destruction fairly soon. Could you possibly expedite this process?"

Kayembe studied the group for a moment.

"Very well, Chief Ramirez. Jax, please prepare the necessary authorizations for my signature."

JAX WILLIAMS WAS at his desk when his comm pinged, signaling an incoming video call. He tapped an icon, and his desktop display came to life with the image of a pixie-faced young woman wearing a flowered Asian silk blouse. She smiled with knowing familiarity.

"Hi, Jax."

"Hello, Alyson. How's my favorite snoopy reporter doing today?"

She gave him a sly look. "I'm glad to see you, too, Jax. Got a minute?"

"For you, Alyson, always."

"Aww, that's sweet. Say, Jax, I noticed on the governor's public info page she granted protected-site status to an asteroid. Is that true?"

"It is."

"That's kinda unusual for a hunk of space rock."

"Aly, something heavy is going down here. If I promise you an exclusive interview with Governor Kayembe, will you hold off on publicizing this for a few days? Please?"

"Say pretty please and I'll think about it."

"Pretty please. Begging, groveling, pretty please."

She gave him a sly grin.

"How can I say no to that? OK, Jax, but don't keep me waiting. I'll be in touch."

The screen went black. Jax closed his eyes and groaned.

THE AZ RECORDS clerk, James Lawrence, sat in his office cubicle processing data files when a shadow loomed from behind. He glanced back over his shoulder to see Bernie Grant standing behind him. Lawrence checked the security cam output window on his display, then swiveled his chair around and looked up at Bernie.

"Can I help you, Mr. Grant?"

"I expect you can, Lawrence. I need an equipment inventory for an asteroid mine."

"Alright, Mr. Grant. Which mine are you interested in?"

"The one on Asteroid 2060RT2."

Lawrence looked at Bernie for a moment, worked his console, then checked the display.

"Hmm … we're still processing that data, Mr. Grant. It won't be finalized until next week."

"Just give me what you have."

"I'm sorry, Mr. Grant. That's against Division policy."

"Well, make an exception. I need that inventory for some important planning today."

Lawrence shook his head. "I wish I could help, but—"

"Just download the damn file!" Bernie waved his tablet at Lawrence. "It'll be no skin off your ass."

"Mr. Grant, my job could be in jeopardy if—"

Bernie leaned close to Lawrence and stared hard at him.

"I understand you have two children attending the Machado Academy."

Lawrence looked at Bernie with confusion, then shock. Bernie flashed him a brief, feral grin.

"You know, Lawrence, I seem to recall a number of complaints at Machado about your children."

Lawrence's eyes narrowed. "That's impossible. They've both gotten consistently excellent evaluations, and they're very popular with the other kids. If there were complaints, the school administration would have notified me or my wife immediately."

"That could all change very quickly, Lawrence. And you must also know that the Alpha Zubrin Board of Directors manages a scholarship fund, and the Machado Academy depends heavily on that fund. And I'm on the board, Lawrence. Am I getting through to you?"

Lawrence sat back in his swivel chair and closed his eyes. He sighed and held out his hand. Bernie placed his tablet onto Lawrence's upturned palm, and three minutes later, strode out of Lawrence's cubicle, stuffing his tablet into a jacket pocket and grinning.

HANA WAS INSPECTING documents on her workstation when the desktop comm light flashed. She changed display windows, and Jax Williams appeared.

"Good morning, Chief Ramirez."

She gave him a brisk nod. "Good morning, Mr. Williams."

He treated her to a winning smile. "Please, just call me Jax."

"Very well, Jax. Do you have news?"

"I'm happy to report that Governor Kayembe has secured an audience for your group with the Sol System Scientific Council. The attached meeting agenda includes the time and location."

"Jax, that's outstanding! We so appreciate everything you and Governor Kayembe have done to help us. By the way, did you find who leaked the asteroid protection order to the press so soon?"

"We're still looking into that."

She nodded. "OK, Jax. Contact me if the governor needs our help."

Hana inspected the meeting agenda, then tapped her headset mic.

"Terzakian, I've got something to show you." She grinned. "No, not that."

EARTH-SIDE, BY THE end of the twenty-first century, environmental destruction had led to a gravely damaged global ecosystem. Atmospheric degradation and global heating resulted in desertification of vast areas of the planet, rendering them unable to support life of any form. The oceans were gradually turning into titanic sewers. Higher marine animals were extinct outside of zoos, and only primitive organisms survived in the seas. Terrestrial wildlife existed in only in remnant populations in a few places. Extensive swaths of arable land and sources of potable water disappeared. An authoritarian regime attacked neighboring countries with biological agents delivered by drone swarms. This sparked unintended deadly pandemics that, ironically, also decimated the attacker's population. Among the survivors, there was widespread famine, failed attempts at migration, and a die-off in the human population. Belief in the Earth's infinite carrying capacity finally disappeared. Clearly, delusional ideology had failed. This revelation led to a global resolve to confront the worst of humanity's atavistic and maladaptive behavior. But human nature remained intransigent.

Undeniable reality forced the world to acknowledge that salvation lay not with ideological assertion, but with fact-based science. Human colonization of Earth's solar system was undertaken, providing an opportunity to rethink many of the old social and governmental paradigms. This led to the formation of the Sol System Confederation and its crown jewel, The Sol System Scientific Council.

Restoration of Earth's biosphere remains a work in progress with a series of small but significant triumphs. Science is now routinely taught at all levels in public schools. Teachers are no longer shouted down, threatened, and attacked for teaching logic, systematic reasoning, fact-based history, and the scientific method. Religion is now practiced at home or in church, not in the public school system, the court house, or the legislature. These changes have furthered the transformation of popular culture. As one parent observed regarding the role of their religious beliefs, "What do I believe? I believe the world would be a better place if people kept their beliefs to themselves." Another offered: "Me? I don't use the word 'believe'; I prefer the word 'think.'" And a third: "I believe I'll have another beer."

Against the harsh backdrop of reality, the Sol System Scientific Council is widely respected, its policies and judgments accepted. Those questioning the council know to do their homework first. The council receives all input with respectful but firm responses rooted in established facts and rigorous logic. Its ascendance in the public eye gave hope to Pelagic observers, including Avala and Rapunzel. Their favorable reports led to a consensus among the Pelagic people to contact the Sol System culture.

HANA'S DESIGNATION OF the group as 'Team Ellis' went unremarked upon as she led the members into the scientific council conference room. In order, the procession comprised Hana, Avala in her usual disguise, Logan, Rapunzel, and Terzakian. Hana and Terzakian, imposing in their dress uniforms, added a dash of formal authority to the group.

At the far end of the room from the entrance, a theater-sized wall display showed the council logo, followed by text:

Special Meeting:

The Discoveries on Asteroid 2060RT2

On the stage, a few meters from the display, sat five desks facing the audience, each labeled with the name of a Scientific Council member. Below the stage, tables stocked with refreshments attracted browsers from the attendees. Facing the stage were several dozen chairs for the audience, with the first row reserved for special non-council attendees. These included Team Ellis, Governor Kayembe, Jax Williams, and Doctors Magdi El-Said, Ved Rao, and Lauren Chen.

Avala made eye contact with Lauren, who gave her an appraising look and walked over.

"Lauren Chen."

They shook hand.

"Avala Cates. Pleased to meet you, Lauren."

Lauren inspected Avala's name tag. "Team Ellis. What's that?"

Rapunzel edged closer.

"We represent interests in Ellis Habitat. Asteroid 2060RT2 is presently in that jurisdiction."

Lauren looked at her in surprise. "What do you know about 2060RT2?"

"Information is our business," Avala said, "and, as you doubtless know, AZ leaks data like a sieve."

Lauren nodded. "That it does."

A MIDDLE-AGED WOMAN in a conservative business suit went to

the stage podium and tapped the microphone. The room's audio system popped, and the buzzing of conversation trailed off.

Lauren gave Avala a knowing look and then walked to her seat.

"Now that had serious weirdness potential," Logan said, "but you and Rapunzel handled it like pros."

Avala shrugged. "What can I say? When you're good, you're good."

Rapunzel raised an eyebrow at her. "Avala's only character flaw is she's too humble."

"If everyone will please take their seats, we'll begin the meeting. My name is Helen Moir, chair of the Sol System Scientific Council. I'd like to welcome you all to this special meeting. As you know, a significant discovery was recently made on Asteroid 2060RT2. On behalf of the board, I'd like to give special thanks to Delta Sector Governor Zodi Kayembe for bringing this matter to our attention. She certainly has wasted no time in effectively using her new position." She gestured to Kayembe, who nodded and smiled at the audience.

"To begin the presentation, I'd like to introduce Dr. Magdi El-Said, Vice-President of Operations of the Alpha Zubrin Corporation." She gestured to Magdi. He stood and then buttoned his suit jacket and strode to the podium. He nodded to Moir, shot his cuffs, then leaned on the podium toward the microphone.

"Thank you for the introduction, Madam Chair. As you are all doubtless aware, our staff recently made a discovery in one of our asteroid mines." He tapped a podium icon, and an image of the mine interior appeared on the display. He refreshed the display.

"They found this black structure. Soon thereafter, we discovered this." The display refreshed again, and the hexagonal artifact appeared. "We stopped the mining operation and began a thorough examination of the site." He gave the audience a minute to process the images. The room was quiet except for a few whispers.

"To clarify the situation and answer your questions, I'd like to introduce Dr. Ved Rao, head scientist of our R and D division. Ved accuses me of hogging all the attention. That, of course, is not true. I save ten percent for him." He gestured to Ved, who stood, nodded to Magdi, and approached the podium.

Ved turned his dark, probing gaze on the audience and then the council members.

"What are these things? Where are they from?" He paused for effect. "Those and a hundred other questions arise. To find answers, Alpha Zubrin is partnering with the University of Mars and several scientific consultants. This consortium will study these objects and the mine site. It will maintain close contact with the Sol System Scientific Council." Ved gave the council members a nod of acknowledgment. "To head this consortium, the logical choice is Dr. Lauren Chen, field supervisor of our scientific research group." He nodded to Lauren and motioned for her to come up.

Lauren approached the podium and adjusted the microphone.

"It's impossible to convey the sense of excitement and wonder these discoveries have ignited among our staff. But tempering this excitement is a tremendous responsibility, part of which is keeping you informed of our progress. We're setting up a consortium website." She tapped an icon, and a network protocol link appeared on the display. "This is a good time for questions."

Immediately, a hand shot up.

"Dr. Chen, how do you know these things aren't a hoax?"

"They could be. But we don't think so. Consider the expense and technical challenge. Who would have the means and the motive?"

Another hand rose.

"Could they have been left by aliens?"

"We're not sure of anything yet. We don't know what they're made of, and we don't know how they got there. It's possible they're not of terrestrial origin."

"Does that mean not of human origin?"

"Possibly. We think it's unlikely, but we haven't ruled it out."

The audience erupted in agitated chatter. Lauren looked at Moir, and she came to the podium and adjourned the meeting.

THE COUNCIL AND Governor Kayembe retired to a private room while the attendees milled about, snacking and talking. Lauren approached Avala and regarded her with a raised eyebrow.

"Somehow, Avala, I can't shake the suspicion you know something about that artifact that I don't."

"And I see why you're an AZ science supervisor."

Governor Kayembe picked up a drink from the snack table and then walked over to them.

"Ah, the two ladies I want to chat with. I see you've already met. Avala, have you told Dr. Chen about our arrangement?"

Lauren caught her eye. "No, Madam Governor, she hasn't."

"Avala, you can explain it to Dr. Chen better than I can."

"Well, Lauren, the artifact is currently being examined by members of my team—"

"So you're the one who stole it!"

Avala shrugged and gave Lauren a look of bogus innocence. "I prefer the word 'borrow.'"

Kayembe took Lauren's arm.

"Dr. Chen, it was Avala who insisted that you take charge of the new research team."

Lauren's expression was both startled and skeptical. She looked at Avala.

"Maybe I should thank you for that, but I still want my toy back."

"Dr. Chen, Avala also nominated you to replace one of our retiring council members. The council offers you the position, if you accept that as well."

Lauren's eyes widened, then she cast a suspicious look at Avala, a smile spreading across her face.

"You're planning to work me to death, aren't you?"

Avala grinned at her. "If you survive drinks and dinner at my lab."

BHANI, JULIO, AND Floyd filed into the AZ lab lunchroom and took seats. Floyd looked at the other two.

"What's this meeting this about?"

Bhani shrugged. "You know as much as I do. Any guess, Julio?"

He shook his head just as Lauren came in.

"You'll be happy to hear we're going back to Hawkington."

Julio looked at her. "To another jail?"

"I'm sorry about that, Julio. I apologize to all of you for being stuck here, but we needed this lab's equipment. We're moving the rest of the work back to the Hawkington lab, and you can return to your apartments."

"So, there's no longer a concern about us leaking information?"

"Magdi and I never had one, Bhani, but senior management wouldn't take our word for it. He finally convinced them there's no longer an issue, given his plans to release information to the public."

Floyd caught her eye. "When can we leave?"

"As soon as you're ready."

BERNIE SAT IN the Hawkington Tap Room, nursing a pint of ale and munching peanuts, when Karpov's man, Corbett, came into the tavern. Spotting Bernie, Corbett walked over and sat in the empty chair facing him. Corbett caught the bartender's eye, raised his arm and snapped his finger, pointing at the table. The bartender nodded and walked over.

"What will you gentlemen be having?"

"Coffee," Corbett said.

Bernie pushed his empty pint glass forward, nodded, and the bartender picked it up.

"More peanuts, too."

Corbett watched Bernie pull his tablet out of a jacket pocket and set it on the table. A minute later, the drinks and peanuts arrived.

"Mr. Grant, have you good news for Mr. Karpov?"

Bernie took a long pull of ale.

"I have an equipment inventory. I was hoping you could look at it."

With his elbow on the table, Corbett held out his hand, palm up, and snapped his finger. Bernie placed the tablet in his hand. Sipping coffee, Corbett thumbed through the inventory list. After a few minutes, the frown on his face relaxed.

"This is very nice, Mr. Grant. I see you have access to the control module." He noticed Bernie's uncertain look. "You do know what I'm talking about, do you not, Mr. Grant?"

Bernie mopped his forehead with a table napkin. "I'm afraid I don't follow you."

Corbett gazed at him for a moment.

"The control module for the Model 782 boring machine. The one in the mine on 2060RT2."

Bernie reached for his pint and took a sip. Corbett gave him a look of mild irritation.

"Mr. Grant, that control module is state-of-the-art, proprietary, and quite valuable. If you can obtain one, Mr. Karpov will be quite pleased."

Bernie, regaining a bit of composure, nodded and took a mouthful of peanuts. Corbett watched him chew the peanuts, then drain his pint. He set down the empty glass and wiped his lips.

"How pleased might Mr. Karpov be?"

"I think Mr. Karpov might consider delivery of the module as satisfying your obligations, Mr. Grant. If you can deliver it by his deadline."

Corbett stood and walked out of the tavern.

14

AVALA, RAPUNZEL, AND Logan sat on the balcony outside the atrium and gazed at the forest. Logan broke the silence.

"That council meeting was intense. I don't like crowds."

"Overall, I think it went well," Avala said, "despite Lauren's suspicion of me."

"I wouldn't worry. I think you won her over."

She looked at him with surprise. "What? No sarcasm? Are you feeling OK, Logy? Rapunzel, I think he looks a little pale. See if he has a fever."

Rapunzel gave her a wry look.

"The council and governor seemed understanding. I hope our project gets enough support."

"I wonder how secure the mine will be," Logan said.

"I think that may depend on Hana, Terzakian, and us," Avala said. Her comm buzzed. She inspected its interface and began scrolling through a text message, a look of surprise on her face. She closed the comm and stared out into the forest. "That was Pelitat. They have the identity of the visitor. And the visitor wants to meet here with us and our AZ partners. Rapunzel, we have to go pick them up at Pelitat as soon as possible."

Logan sat dumbstruck for a moment. "Why do they want to come here?"

"The visitor has watched the Science Council and Governor Kayembe's actions. The visitor is confident peaceful collaboration is now possible, if security is adequate."

"I don't know how much more boggling my mind can take."

"We'll have plenty of opportunities to find out soon," Rapunzel said, giving him a wink.

Avala caught Rapunzel's eye. "We need to get going."

"What? I can't go?" Logan asked.

Avala looked at him with a pained expression.

"Logan, I really wish you could, but I'm sure you know why you can't."

He gave her a sly look. "You actually thought that was a serious question. How touching."

She narrowed her eyes at him. "Rapunzel, you can skip taking his temperature."

"Noted. I'll contact the air taxi."

"How long will you two be gone?"

"We should be back tomorrow," Avala said. "How will you amuse yourself while we're away?"

"I certainly don't intend to sit here while you're gone. Hawkington is plenty amusing, and I can bring Lauren up to speed. Anything I should or should not tell her?"

"Excellent idea. She has to know everything for our collaboration to work."

"OK, then. I'll ride over to the transport terminal with you two, then catch the Hawkington shuttle. Try not to destroy too many rigs on your way to Pelitat."

Avala looked at Rapunzel.

"I just thought of an alternative medical procedure you could administer to Logy."

LAUREN WAS IN her Hawkington office when a tapping sounded, and she saw Logan in the doorway.

"Logan, good to see you. Come on in." She gestured to a chair.

"Avala and Rapunzel are on their way to Pelitat to pick up someone I know you'll want to meet."

She gave him a bemused look. "And who might that be?"

"The individual who left the artifact on 2060RT2."

She straightened up in her seat, her eyes wide.

"You're kidding, right?"

"And that individual is not human."

She studied him for a moment.

"Something tells me you're not kidding."

"They'll probably return to Avala's lab in the morning. You may want to arrange transport over there tomorrow."

"Like hell! I am not waiting here until tomorrow. I'll ride back there with you tonight."

"Alrighty then. Meet me at the transport terminal in two hours."

ON TURING HABITAT in Gamma Sector, Artie Kresse sat in her Burwell Solutions office. She was studying her desk display when Bernie Grant appeared in the doorway, staring at her.

"I'm Bernard Grant, from the Alpha Zubrin Corporation board of directors."

Under bushy, beetling black eyebrows, his bulging eyes, scowling face, and imposing bulk gave the intimidation he relied upon. Now they had no apparent effect.

The compact, uniformed young woman sitting before him inspected him with large, calm blue eyes. Her cherubic face radiated the strength and confidence of one who had seen far too much for her age. She pushed a stray wisp of flaming-red hair away from her densely freckled cheek, then stood and extended her hand.

"Arthuryn Kresse. What can I do for you, Mr. Grant?"

He lowered himself into a chair and inspected her.

"I'm here to engage your services." He folded his hands across his belly and looked around the office.

She tapped a console icon, then looked back at him. "And those would be ...?"

"Transportation to a certain location and technical services."

She glanced at her console again and pecked an icon.

"Where is this location and what technical services do you need, Mr. Grant?"

His chair creaked ominously as he leaned back, folded his arms, and scrutinized her with an imperious scowl.

"At this time, those details are confidential."

"Mr. Grant, before we can go any further here, I need those details."

A brief flash of uncertainty crossed Bernie's imperious face.

"I'm on the board of directors of the Alpha Zubrin Corporation," he said with tentative finality. He tilted his head back and inspected her reaction.

"You already told me, Mr. Grant."

"And as per my position there, I have an interest in protecting the assets of said corporation."

She closed her eyes and rubbed her forehead. Picking up a stylus, she began tapping it on the desk in between glances at the wall clock. He glared at her.

"I'm sorry! Am I boring you?"

She gazed at him with lowered eyelids.

"Mr. Grant, I need to know exactly where, and for what, you need our services."

"On 2060RT2. That's an—"

"Asteroid." She leaned forward and inspected his face. "Currently in Delta Sector, and currently protected. No doubt a coincidence. Why do you want to go there and what services you need?"

"I need to inspect and secure the mine site."

"Isn't that a job for regular AZ staff?"

"Under normal circumstances, perhaps."

She settled back in her chair, a hint of amusement playing at the corners of her mouth.

"What abnormal circumstances require the involvement of an AZ board member?"

"Due to an error, certain proprietary devices were left unsecured at the mine site. I have reason to believe that an Alpha Zubrin executive intends to take these devices from the asteroid and sell them to a competitor. I'm going to prevent that."

"Again, isn't that a job for AZ technical and security staff? I'm not clear on Burwell's role here."

Beads of sweat emerged on Bernie's forehead.

"AZ staff can't be trusted. I intend to retrieve the devices and arrange proper inventory and storage."

"I see. So, once you get these devices, which AZ warehouse will they be taken to?"

He wiped his face with a handkerchief. "I'll handle that."

She gazed at him, her skepticism palpable.

"So, in summary, Mr. Grant, you want Burwell to help you trespass on a protected site, remove proprietary AZ property, and take it to an unspecified location, all without informing any AZ personnel. Am I correct, Mr. Grant?"

He looked at her with a startled expression.

"Mr. Grant, I think you misunderstand the nature of Burwell's business. We're done here."

MAGDI'S DESK COMM buzzed. "Magdi, Lauren is here."

"OK, Jan. Send her in."

Lauren wore a casual business pants suit, her hair tied back. She glanced at Magdi as she went over to the coffee counter and poured a cup. He watched her, twiddling a stylus through his fingers. She brought her coffee over and sat near his desk, sipping the coffee and regarding him in silence.

Magdi sat back, lacing his fingers behind his head and gazing at her.

"Something's up," he observed, giving her an inquiring look.

She inspected him and sipped her coffee. "Oh, is it ever."

He closed his eyes and sighed. "OK, let's have it."

"Logan Rhodes just dropped the granddaddy of all bombshells on me."

"And?"

"Avala's got connections with the visitor to 2060RT2, who cut the hole in the tube and left the artifact in the mine. And with the visitor's people."

Magdi sat up. "What people?"

"Do you recall our discussion with Ved regarding a particular possibility about the visitor?"

"Get to the point."

"Occam's razor?" she observed him with arched eyebrows.

His eyes widened as he sat back, loosened his tie, and stared at her.

"And Avala wants us—you, me, and Ved—to meet the visitor," she said, "at Avala's lab."

Magdi's eyes narrowed with skepticism.

"I'm serious, Magdi. It's time for show and tell. Are you up for it?"

He watched her for a moment. "OK. When is this meeting?"

"In the next few days."

LOGAN CAME DOWN the walkway to the shuttle terminal, where Lauren was pacing back and forth near the boarding ramp. She saw him and strode over.

"It leaves in ten minutes," she said. "Let's get on board. I already paid the fare."

"Let's find seats in the rear. I believe I hear a gin and tonic calling my name."

THE FLIGHT LANDED at Ellis Habitat, and Lauren and Logan exited the shuttle.

"We need to keep Hana and Terzakian in the loop," he said. "They'll be handling security."

They headed up the walk toward the Ellis Health and Safety compound. As they approached Hana's office, the nameplate on her door caught their attention.

Hana Ramirez, Group Supervisor

Hana was reading documents on her display when Logan knocked on her door frame. She glanced up and smiled. "Logan, good to see you."

Lauren stepped around him and made eye contact with Hana.

"Dr. Chen! What a surprise!" Hana gestured to the empty seats in front of her desk.

"Just Lauren, Hana. I'm not big on titles."

"Alright, Lauren. I'm guessing you two have something interesting to discuss."

"Congratulations on the promotion," Logan said.

"Thanks, but it may soon turn into a mixed blessing."

"How so?" Lauren asked.

"I'm in charge of coordinating security for 2060RT2 with the other sectors. The Confederation is supporting us, but it's still going to be tough. I'm not sure I'm capable of the required diplomacy."

"And that's one of the many reasons they wouldn't put me on that job," Lauren said.

They turned and saw Terzakian leaning against the doorframe with his characteristic grin.

Hana looked at him and pointed at a chair.

"Come in and have a seat. Terzakian will handle things here when I'm out on other business."

"Hana, Avala's lab is going to be a busy place," Lauren said. "I'm sorry to add to your problems, but security there may soon be an issue."

"I'm taking that into account. We'll have plenty of resources on hand, so I wouldn't worry about it."

"I'll toddle over occasionally to see how things are going," Terzakian said.

"We'll always be glad to see you there," Logan said.

LOGAN AND LAUREN stepped out of the air taxi at Avala's lab and walked into the atrium. She paused, looked around, and nodded with approval.

"Nice."

"I'll show you where your room is."

Logan led her to the upstairs apartment corridor and pointed at several closed doors.

"Take your pick." He turned and headed back down the stairs.

He was standing by the atrium's glass wall checking his tablet when Lauren came down the stairs and walked over.

"When are they supposed to be here?"

"I'm checking for an update right now. See if they sent you anything."

She took out her tablet and worked the interface. "Nothing yet."

"Let's go check the comm terminal."

Lauren followed Logan into the data room. He pointed to the consoles and displays.

"Most of the work is done here." He checked the data room terminal for messages. "Nothing yet."

"I really hope no news is good news."

"We would have gotten a message if anything had gone wrong. Let's get something to eat."

OUTSIDE THE LAB, a distant ring of overhead lights brightened and dimmed in a daily sequence. Now it was as dark as it ever got on Ellis Habitat. They sat in the atrium, picking at bowls of vegetables.

"Logan, how long have you been here?"

He thought for a second. "About ten days. Why?"

"What do you do here?"

"I'm renting space to run my consulting business."

"What kind of consulting?"

"Financial and IT advising, mainly for small businesses."

"How did you wind up here?"

He looked at her for a moment.

"It's complicated."

"Isn't everything?"

"Look at how you wound up here."

"Good point. It's been a weird road for both of us. How well do you know Avala and Rapunzel?"

"About as well as possible in ten days."

"In other words, you don't know them."

"I've been around them under a variety of circumstances."

"Enough to draw any tentative conclusions?"

Logan thought for a moment. "Yes, from subjective impressions. Personally, I like them both."

"Do you trust them?"

"That would depend on specifics. Maybe."

"Do you know anything about their backgrounds?"

He frowned in concentration. "Nothing I can verify. I found this place by accident. Since I've been here, I haven't found any clear factual information on either of them."

"Doesn't that worry you?"

"Not really. You'll see why when you get to know them. How long are you planning to stay?"

"I'm not, for any extended period. Between my labs in Hawkington and Penrose, I'm booked solid."

He looked around the atrium, waving his fork. "And now Avala's lab makes three."

"I keep reminding myself this will be interesting."

"I hope for your sake you don't have an over-active imagination."

"Nope. A normal one, which is quite enough."

"Worst-case scenario?"

"Logan, I don't want to go there."

"Not if you want to get any sleep tonight."

"Tonight? You mean last night." She pointed at the wall clock. "For me, sleep is off the table."

"Well, I'm going to try. I don't do well without sleep."

He went to the sink, rinsed his bowl, then headed up to his room.

15

DOWNSTAIRS, LOGAN FOUND Lauren in the atrium, pacing with a coffee cup, and the smell of toasted bread in the air. She stopped pacing and looked at him.

"Well, sleeping beauty arises."

He yawned and waved absently at her as he shuffled to the kitchen. Carrying the coffeepot and a stack of toast, he headed to the balcony.

Lauren followed, then sat opposite him at the table and began checking her tablet.

"Damn."

"No messages?"

"No. What about you?"

He pulled his tablet over and tapped the screen.

"Nope, but I've learned to not expect anything, especially with Avala and Rapunzel." She gave him a quizzical look. "They like to mess with your head. They'll make you pry information out of them just for grins. They like games. You'll see."

"Well, I'm not in the mood for games this morning."

"I don't think they'll be, either, considering who or what they're bringing with them."

Lauren's comm buzzed. Avala's text message got right to the point:

Inbound. ETA 1 hour. Get Magdi, Ved, and Hana.

Lauren stared at the message, then began working her comm.

A FEW MINUTES later, an air taxi deposited Hana at the lab entrance.

"Lauren, I got your message. I gather this is important."

"Avala and Rapunzel are on their way here with someone you should meet."

Hana looked around the lab.

"I've seen drone images of this place, but I've never seen it up close or been inside."

"How many people know about this facility?" Logan asked.

"That's not clear. Ellis admin is good about respecting privacy, and it keeps a well-secured database. All I found on this lab is the title history and a record of prompt assessment payments."

"How secure is this lab?" Lauren asked.

"Well, it's isolated and not on most maps. Besides that, I don't know."

"What kinds of trouble might we be facing here?" Logan asked.

"Organized crime, psychotics, political operatives, nosy neighbors, you name it. The trick is to identify them, assess the threat and likelihood, then list them in decreasing order of expected damage. The Scientific Council gave me a budget, so that will dictate what gets done to some extent. What will you do here, Lauren?"

"That depends on who Avala and Rapunzel bring with them."

AVALA, STILL IN disguise, Rapunzel, and a figure wearing a gray hooded cloak exited the air taxi. They walked to the atrium and paused in the entrance. Avala stepped inside, looking at Logan, Hana, and Lauren. She gestured to the cloaked figure.

"This is Zareemet."

The stranger entered, pulled back the hood, then removed the cloak and laid it on a chair. She wore a dark blue tunic patterned with gold piping, conventional buttons, and matching pants. Her shoes were dark and substantial, revealing little of her foot structure. She carried a green satchel with a shoulder strap. Around her neck was a tube carrying gas from a container in the satchel. An extension along her right cheek delivered the gas to her nostrils.

Zareemet had pale, nearly translucent skin, and fine, white, shoulder-length hair. Her eyes were wide and nearly colorless. She had no eyebrows. Her facial features were human in appearance. Except for an open and curious look, her expressions were unreadable as she gazed around the lab. Her ample but otherwise unremarkable lips parted to reveal many small, fine, white teeth. Her build was slight but not petite, and clearly female by human standards.

Avala looked around the group. "She is eager to talk with you."

Zareemet smiled at them, then spoke into a mic attached to the gas tube. Her words came through a small speaker clipped to her tunic. Zareemet's natural voice was soft, her language obscure, including various clicks, buzzes, and chirps that an ordinary person would be hard-pressed to understand, much less duplicate.

"It is an honor to meet you and to visit your wonderful world. Thank you for inviting me and accepting me as a representative of my people."

Avala caught her eye. "Everyone here feels honored and excited to meet you, Zareemet."

They all turned at the whirring of an air taxi approaching the lab. It landed on the helipad, and out stepped Magdi and Ved, buttoning their suit jackets and looking around as they strode to the atrium's entrance. Avala waved them in, and they stood, looking at the group, their gaze coming to rest on Zareemet. Avala walked over to them.

"We're just beginning the introductions. Her name is Zareemet."

They nodded and approached her.

"I am Magdi El-Said. I am honored to meet you, Zareemet." He held out his hand and Zareemet, apparently briefed by Avala on Sol System courtesy protocols, extended her slender, pale hand. She repeated the ritual with everyone except Avala and Rapunzel, and they all stood in a moment of awkwardness, gazing at one another. Avala whispered something to Zareemet, and she spoke into her translator.

"My people have observed developments in your star system."

"What have they concluded?" Magdi asked.

"That we can establish a peaceful and productive friendship."

"Such an outcome would bring joy to my people," Ved said.

"And ours as well, Ved."

Avala looked around at the gathering.

"She's a scientist, not a diplomat. The translator is limited, so I'll be helping her."

Avala whispered a prompt to Zareemet.

"Can you tell me, Ved, what measures you are prepared to undertake to ensure our friendship?"

He nodded. "Our consortium represents an association of

scientists and builders. We garner wide respect and trust among our people and command substantial resources. My colleagues and I can access the consortium's resources in order to ensure a peaceful collaboration. And your people?"

Avala whispered another brief prompt to Zareemet.

"For many generations, we have wandered the galaxy. We are drawn spiritually to worlds such as we once had, now lost to a dying star. Avala has shown Logan glimpses of that world, through the device she calls the artifact. My people seek a new home world, and perhaps you could help us survive until we find one. We have much to offer, scientifically and technologically. We will be valuable allies."

Magdi and Ved exchanged glances, then looked at Lauren. She caught Zareemet's eye.

"Zareemet, ever since I was a small child, I have dreamed of meeting you, of becoming your friend, and of exploring the mysteries of the universe with you."

Avala whispered to Zareemet. She looked at Lauren and gave her a beguiling smile.

"Then you and I, Lauren, are very much alike."

"Zareemet, tell us how your people decided to contact the Sol System culture," Rapunzel said.

"Our scientists predicted the similarities of our worlds made it likely yours would be inhabited by sentient beings with a morphology and intelligence enabling productive communication. They appear to have been correct.

"Monitoring your electromagnetic communications led some in our culture to question the nature of your people. They advised we remain at the edge of your system and avoid detection until we learned more. We have now seen enough to conclude that we can undertake a peaceful collaboration." She gave Avala an uncertain look, and they exchanged brief whispers.

"The waning of warfare since your twenty-first century, the ascendance of your new age of science, your resurrection of Earth's biosphere, and the colonization of your star's system have given us hope. The star of our home world underwent a gradual change over many generations of our people. This led to the eventual collapse of our home world's biosphere. Fortunately, our technology enabled us to escape on a fleet of vessels. You can appreciate the magnitude of the tragedy, losing our world, once as beautiful and verdant as yours. At one point, we feared your world would suffer a similar fate, albeit for a different reason. But you gained sufficient collective awareness and technological advance to prevent the irreversible collapse of your biosphere." She consulted Avala then continued.

"Your structure of cooperative but autonomous sectors seems likely to avoid malignant aggregations of power. Previous governments tended to concentrate power and often culminated in tyranny and systematic violence. Your Scientific Council and Confederation, while limited to the power of persuasion, are respected and supported by your people. We hope and trust our positive conclusions about you are correct, as we are now vulnerable to hostile actions by your people."

Magdi nodded to her. "We will do what we can to assist you, Zareemet. For the immediate future, however, it will be best if you remain hidden. We can't yet predict how some members of our culture will react to you. Ved and I are gradually releasing information to our media in a manner fostering public acceptance of your presence. For now, however, the matter is delicate."

Zareemet consulted with Avala and turned to Magdi.

"I understand, Magdi, and I am grateful on behalf of my people for any help you can give us."

"Zareemet, can you tell us why you went into the asteroid mine?"

"Of course, Ved. I was tending to a research project in the asteroid's cave before your people installed the mine infrastructure. I was alarmed when I discovered it, fearing for our primordia, organisms we cultivate as specialized workers for environments such as your Asteroid 2060RT2. We also recognize the asteroid's rich mineral deposits, but did not expect your interest when we began work there. I arrived at the asteroid to care for our primordia, but found the cave entrance blocked by your mine enclosure. I could not determine the entrance protocol and could not open it. Time was short, so I forced an entry, minimizing damage to your structure."

"Zareemet, were you concerned about encountering our miners?"

"Of course, Hana. But I decided the risk was acceptable. I was alone and would present myself peacefully. Your miners appeared to understand and did not confront me. It required three visits to extract the primordia from that chamber. There are more, deeper in the asteroid's crust. On my last visit, I found your miner's gift, and I left one in return."

"That is a remarkable sequence of events, Zareemet. We are lucky nothing went wrong."

"Your people, Hana, are perceptive, and we are grateful for your cooperation and help." Zareemet turned to Lauren. "We would like very much to continue our primordia research and development, with your participation, of course. The primordia would help both of our cultures."

Magdi looked at Lauren. "Your show."

"Not just mine. Hana, Avala, and Logan will be essential."

Logan gave Lauren a surprised glance.

"Zareemet, can you tell us more about your gift, the artifact?"

"Yes, Logan. It is an education and training device for our children and primordia. I altered the one I left for you to include information about our people and our history. I hope you find it interesting."

"We are fascinated, but struggling to access its information. We need to learn how your people transcended the ignorance, hate, and violence that has plagued us throughout our history."

Zareemet gazed at Logan for a moment, then consulted with Avala.

"We've been observing your culture for some time, Logan, and we've been both repelled and intrigued by glimpses of our own distant past. We welcome the opportunity to share what we have learned about removing the tragic sequence of ignorance, fear, hate, and violence from our culture. There are reasons for optimism among your people, and we can explore them."

"How do your people refer to your culture? Do you have a name for it?"

"The closest English translation, Hana, would be like 'travelers of the universe,' 'wanderers of the heavens,' or 'stellar gypsies,' but we prefer the pelagic people, sailing on a sea of stars."

"Zareemet, what is your relationship with Pelitat?"

"Lauren, it is much like your relationship to your Alpha Zubrin Corporation."

"Are you an employee of Pelitat?"

"More like what you call a consultant, sharing common interests in science, concern for our people, and hope for them and others." Zareemet turned to Magdi. "What is your organization, this Alpha Zubrin Corporation, prepared to do in cooperation with us?"

"I can assure you, Zareemet, our governing board will be most cooperative. They understand, or soon will, how important that is. Perhaps you and Team Ellis can compile a list of cooperation points, along with your associated requirements. I will present it to the corporation's board of directors."

Ved gave Zareemet a sly look. "Behold the level of authority Magdi assumes."

She gave Avala an uncertain look, and Avala whispered something to her. She emitted a strange, musical laugh and smiled at Ved and Magdi.

THE SOL SYSTEM attendees departed, and Rapunzel took Zareemet back to Pelitat. Avala, Lauren, and Logan sat on the balcony nursing drinks and tossing treats to the tree creatures as dusk descended inside Ellis Habitat. Avala shifted her eyes to Logan.

"Well, Logy, now you certainly can't say you're bored."

"When did I ever say that? Lauren, do you think this place is boring?"

"I'm just waiting for my head to stop spinning."

Logan looked at Avala.

"Babe, I don't think her head is spinning enough. Why don't you wipe off that makeup?"

Lauren's eyes narrowed, and she looked at Avala. "What is he talking about?"

Avala gave Logan a sideways look. "I'll get you for this, Logy."

She began wiping the makeup off with a small towel. As she removed the brown, her gold-spangled blue skin emerged. Lauren's eyes widened as she watched.

"Wow. I've seen some far-out skin work, but ..."

"I guess it's time for you to see the real me."

Logan regarded them with amusement as he sipped his drink. "And don't forget the eyes."

She removed her contact lenses and gazed at Lauren with her bright emerald orbs.

Shaking her head, Lauren sighed and gave Avala and Logan a weary look.

"I think exhaustion has finally caught up with me, and I'm actually in my apartment now, sound asleep, and today has all been a dream."

"I know the feeling," Logan said.

Avala removed the wig and shook out her sapphire braids. Amusement tugged at the corners of her lips, now their usual violet. "No dream, Lauren."

Lauren's eyes widened as she inspected Avala more closely. "Are you from ..."

"Yes, Lauren, the Pelagic culture. Rapunzel is, too."

"What about you, Logan? What star system are you from?"

"Sol System." He shrugged. "So boring."

Rapunzel smiled at her. "Welcome to the lab, Lauren."

AVALA AND LOGAN were sitting on the balcony, chatting and poking at their tablets, when Rapunzel marched out.

"We've got a problem."

Avala looked up and sighed. "What is it now?"

"Lately, I've focused the lab's snooping tech on sector comm traffic. It's pieced together some interesting intelligence."

Logan looked at her. "And?"

"A reporter for News-Blaster just put up a feed-blurb about the sector governor granting protected status to 2060RT2. It mentioned this is the first uninhabited asteroid to get that designation."

"So? Who's likely to care?"

"It gets worse. This morning, I picked up more chatter involving 2060RT2's coordinates."

"So? I would expect the mine's still on some AZ back burner."

"And about to be moved to someone's front burner, it seems. An AZ board member named Bernard Grant just hired a contractor who engages in trespass, theft, and trafficking in controlled substances. Chatter includes acquisition of high-yield explosives by Grant's contractor. This may or may not be coincidental."

"I don't assume coincidence."

Rapunzel looked at him and nodded.

"Grant appears to be planning a trip to the asteroid. He said in one message he thinks the vice-president of operations, Magdi El-Said, is going to steal equipment from the site. That alone would make little sense, but Grant and El-Said have a well-documented history of mutual animosity. El-Said openly refers to Grant as 'Board Genius' and does not hide his contempt for him. I suspect Grant is the one planning the theft."

"What leads you to that conclusion?"

"Simple psychology. Often, what your opponent accuses you of is precisely what they are doing. Someone in El-Said's position and with his reputation is highly unlikely to engage in such an activity."

Logan looked at her with alarm. "Why would Grant use explosives?"

"In attempting to cover his tracks. Destruction of the mine would conceal the theft, but only briefly, which would be consistent with Grant's history of poor judgment."

"We have to assume he's planning this," Avala said. "We've got to keep him off that asteroid."

"Yes. An explosion at the site could kill Zareemet's primordia."

"Ellis Health and Safety has law-enforcement authority there," Logan said, "at least while the asteroid's in Delta Sector."

"Which is why we need to contact Hana and Terzakian immediately," Rapunzel said. "The chatter indicates Grant and company are going there tomorrow morning."

SITTING IN HIS Ellis H&S office, Terzakian was scrolling through robot technical manuals when Hana tapped on his doorframe.

"A situation. Some nasty little characters are planning a trip to 2060RT2."

He gave her a puzzled look. "And we know this how?"

"Rapunzel picked up the comm chatter, and she, Avala, and Logan want to roll on it now."

"How?"

"Avala's got a Cobra Mark Ten."

His eyes widened and then narrowed with intrigue. "Where?"

"Right here on Ellis. I deputized all three of them."

A grin spread across his face.

"You think they can handle it? If they get in over their heads, they'll be on their own."

"Rapunzel sent me footage of Avala piloting the Cobra in action. She won't say, but I think Avala has military training. With luck, we won't have any space garbage to explain when she's done."

"Hopefully, it won't come to that."

"Or it could serve as a useful example."

"Oh, now Chief, that's just cold."

16

IN THE HAWKINGTON transport terminal, Bernie Grant hauled his considerable bulk into the Sidewinder's cockpit and flopped into the copilot's seat. Behind him, two passengers sat stone-faced as the pilot climbed in and worked the control interface. Bernie looked back at them.

"Perkins, did you load the tools for removing the module?"

"Yes, Mr. Grant."

"Ferrell, what about you? Did you bring the explosives?"

"Yup."

The pilot glared at Bernie and held out his hand.

"Grant, I need those coordinates. Now."

Bernie grudgingly handed over a data stick.

"I expect you to purge them from your system once we get there."

"Yeah, yeah. What's going on out there, anyhow?"

"That's confidential, and liability-wise, the less you know, the better."

The pilot shrugged, then tapped a few icons, and the Sidewinder got underway.

IN THE PRIVATE craft wing of the Ellis terminal, Avala powered up the Cobra's systems. Rapunzel strapped into the copilot's seat and Logan climbed into a third seat installed behind them. Rapunzel programmed the ship's AI while Avala checked the flight data and weapons systems. She turned and gave Logan a worried look.

"I wish you'd stayed at the lab."

"Are you kidding? I wouldn't miss this for anything."

"Logan, I don't want anything to happen to you."

"I feel the same way about you."

Rapunzel cleared her throat.

"Could you two please cut the melodramatic blather? I'm trying to concentrate."

Logan caught Avala's eye. "Easily distracted, isn't she?"

"We're going to have to pour on the coals," Rapunzel said. "They have an hour's head start."

THE SIDEWINDER SETTLED onto the 2060RT2 landing area, and the pilot adjusted the engines to idle.

Bernie looked at the passengers behind him.

"It's time for you two to earn your fees. Let's do this and get out of here."

Perkins and Ferrell unbuckled from their seats and prepared to exit the Sidewinder through the craft's airlock. Wearing pressure suits, they carried their equipment to the mine entrance and went through the front hatch.

"Unlocked front hatch. Not much for security here," Perkins said to Ferrell through his suit comm.

"So, AZ will only have itself to blame when we blow it."

They walked past the crew's quarters to the mine. Ferrell set down his equipment and began preparing the explosives while Perkins continued toward the boring machine.

THE SIDEWINDER PILOT inspected his control and scanning interfaces, and Bernie fidgeted between glances at the cockpit clock.

"How long is this going to take?"

"That's not my department. I'm just a high-priced taxi driver."

The cabin speaker crackled.

"Mr. Grant, Perkins here. The module is not in the machine."

"What?"

"The module's not here, sir. It's been removed."

Bernie's his arrogant sneer was now a twisted rictus of fury.

"No! That can't be!"

"Mr. Grant, look at your display."

The cam image showed the machine's side where the module should have been.

Bernie's face contorted into a grotesque mask of fear as he stared at the display. He began to perspire, and soon a sour odor filled the cabin.

Ferrell's voice came over the speaker.

"Grant, do you want to cancel the blow?"

Bernie glared at the display, his face reddening.

"No! Continue as planned!"

A few minutes later, Perkins cleared the Sidewinder's airlock and entered the cabin.

"Mr. Grant, I'm real sorry about—"

"Shut the fuck up!"

IN THE COBRA'S cockpit, they watched the asteroid's image grow larger on their displays. Rapunzel broke the silence.

"Avala, it appears the craft has landed near the mine."

"We have to confront them now, before they do any damage. Approach and hover so they can see that we mean business."

Rapunzel nodded and worked her flight sticks.

"Ship, deploy hard points."

"Acknowledged, Commander."

THE SIDEWINDER PILOT stared at his hull cam display.

"Grant, we've got company. Check your display."

"What?" Bernie attempted to rotate his corpulent frame in his seat. "Who?"

"I have no idea. As I recall, you said this business was confidential."

Bernie watched his display as the Cobra descended fifty meters away.

"Get us out of here! Now! Go!"

"Ferrell is still in the mine."

"I don't care! Get us out of—"

The cabin speaker popped, and Avala's voice came on.

"Sidewinder, shut down your engines. That is not a request."

The pilot inspected his console and opened a comm channel.

"Cobra, this is the Sidewinder pilot speaking. Identify yourself and your purpose here."

On his display, he watched the Cobra bring its hard points to bear on the Sidewinder. He stared wide-eyed at Bernie, who gaped at the Cobra on his display.

Avala tapped her headset mic.

"Sidewinder, you are in a restricted area, and I'll be asking the questions."

The pilot and Bernie stared at their displays as a laser beam flashed in front of the Sidewinder, sending up a plume of dust and debris.

"Jesus Christ! Grant, what the hell have you gotten us into?"

"Sidewinder," Avala said, "are you getting the picture?"

"This is Bernard Grant! Of the Alpha Zubrin Corporation! You are interfering with the official business of the Alpha Zubrin Corporation! I demand that you break off immediately!"

The cabin speaker popped. "Sidewinder, do you have people in the mine?"

"That's none of your—"

"Shut up, Grant," the pilot said, glaring at Bernie with disgust. "Affirmative, Cobra. We have one man in there now."

"Sidewinder, instruct your man to place his weapons on the deck three meters away, sit down, and raise his hands. We will be armed when we approach. Send us your local comm frequency."

"Ferrell, did you copy that?"

"Yup. Tell them not to shoot; I'm sitting tight."

"Rapunzel, keep an eye on those turkeys," Avala said, unbuckling from her seat.

Logan looked at her. "What's the plan?"

"Drag Ferrell out of the mine and take them all to Zebra Station."

"I'm going with you."

"OK." She retrieved two laser carbines from a locker.

Logan looked at her with raised eyebrows. "Seriously?"

"They must know that we mean business, Logan, and I'm not taking any chances."

"Do you understand the shit-rain that will come down if we use these things?"

She ignored his question and handed him a carbine.

AVALA AND LOGAN walked past the crew quarters and found Ferrell sitting on a crate, his hands held high. At his feet lay a large, black satchel. Avala adjusted their suit comm channel to the Sidewinder crew's frequency.

"Logan, watch him. If he moves, shoot him."

Logan raised his carbine and took aim at Ferrell.

Avala approached him. "Where's the weapon?"

"No weapon."

"Where are the explosives?"

"Here." Ferrell pointed to the satchel at his feet.

"Is that all of them?"

"Yes."

"If you're lying, I will put you down. On your feet."

Ferrell stood, his hands still raised.

"Pick up the bag." She motioned toward it with the muzzle of her carbine.

"Sidewinder, we're coming out with your man. Open your cargo bay hatch."

"Acknowledged," the pilot said.

Avala and Logan marched Ferrell out to the Sidewinder.

She motioned toward the Sidewinder's open hatch.

"Get in."

He stepped inside the cargo bay, set down the bag of explosives, and sat on it as the hatch closed.

"Sidewinder, we are sending you vector coordinates," Avala said. "Follow them and dock per instructions received en route. Is that clear?"

"Crystal," the pilot said.

Logan and Avala cleared the Cobra's airlock and settled into their seats.

"Rapunzel, arrange docking at Zebra Station for our new friends, with deluxe accommodations courtesy of Ellis H and S."

"With pleasure, Avala."

LAUREN WAS IN her Hawkington lab, working on research plans, when her desk comm pinged.

Avala's face appeared on the display.

"Lauren, new developments. Bernie Grant is under house arrest for trespass and attempted theft at Site 1287."

Her eyes widened. "What?"

"Rapunzel has been following sector comm traffic, and she knew something was brewing. We nailed him and his hired crew at the asteroid."

"What was he after?"

"One of his crew told us he wanted the control module from the boring machine. It's worth a lot of money on the black market."

"That son of a bitch!"

"If that's not bad enough, he was also going to destroy the mine with explosives to hide the theft."

Lauren stared at the display, shaking her head.

BERNIE PACED AROUND his luxurious suite, staring out the glass wall at the winking lights of Hawkington and the blackness of night looming beyond. He twisted the ankle monitor and swore to himself as he tried to shift it to a comfortable position. If he tried to remove the device, it would deliver a searing electrical jolt and notify the authorities. Even if he succeeded, escape from Hawkington was unlikely.

His comm buzzed, and he stared wide-eyed at it for a moment before answering.

"Mr. Corbett, I—"

With the comm to his ear, he staggered to a plush sofa and collapsed, his mouth quivering.

"Mr. Corbett, it's still possible to obtain the module! I know who—"

He listened, trembling, as he mopped sweat from his face and neck.

"Bhanupriya Oka! She's on the mine crew! They must have taken it! She knows who has it!"

He listened a few moments longer.

"Yes, Mr. Corbett, I understand." He shut off his comm, dropped it onto the floor, and buried his face in a sofa cushion.

BHANI TOOK THE stairs up to her Hawkington apartment. When she reached the landing outside her door, a man stepped from the shadows, grabbed her, and put his hand over her mouth. She struggled, then felt the sting of a needle in her hip. She grew weak and lost consciousness.

Ascending through a dense fog, Bhani was vaguely aware of

lying on her sofa. Somehow, the notion struck her as uproariously funny, and she giggled.

"Wow, this couch is so comfortable!"

The man sitting in the chair next to the couch smiled benevolently at her.

"Yes, Bhanupriya, it is."

Her mind floated through a haze into clarity.

Only mom calls me Bhanupriya.

The man was illuminated by a small kitchen lamp.

She rolled her head to the side and gave him a lazy grin.

"Who are you?"

"I'm Mike, Bhanupriya. Don't you remember?"

She yawned and giggled.

"No."

"That's all right. It will all come back to you."

"All of what?"

"The mine, Bhanupriya, tell me about the mine."

"What part of it?"

"There were some big machines. Tell me about the big machines."

"There were lots of big machines, Mike."

"There was one called the borer. Tell me about it."

"The technicians handled that. I did other things."

"What kinds of things?"

I don't know anyone named Mike.

"I'm thirsty, Mike. I need a glass of water."

She tried to sit up, and Mike got the water from the kitchen.

"You must have heard them talk about the machine, Bhanupriya."

I don't think I should tell you.

"No. We all just did our jobs. We didn't talk about them much."

"But someone must have mentioned a control module. Think, Bhanupriya. What did they say about the control module?"

The fog was clearing.

I don't like this.

"I'm sleepy now, Mike."

She turned away and closed her eyes, listening to Mike drum his fingers on the chair arms.

Knocking sounded on the apartment door.

"Bhani? Are you there?"

Mike was quiet, and a minute later, the knocking stopped.

Julio walked back down the stairs. Taking his comm from a jacket pocket, he called Lauren's lab.

"Lauren, is Bhani there?"

"No. She left a little while ago. Isn't she in her apartment?"

"She's not there. We were going out this evening. Any idea where she might be?"

"Julio, come over to the lab."

"I'm on my way," he said, tapping Floyd's number on his comm.

Lauren's lab was a short walk from the apartment. She was waiting at the entrance.

"I called Floyd," Julio said. "He doesn't know where she would be."

"Julio, last week, Bernard Grant came here demanding to see her. He gave no reason, but it must have something to do with 2060RT2. I told him she was unavailable. He was acting strangely. Or not; he's a weird guy. If he had a legitimate reason to talk to her—"

"He'd have told you. Lauren, this smells bad."

"Grant was arrested with a crew trying to steal the boring machine control module. He was going to destroy the mine with explosives."

Julio stared at her for a moment. "How would Bhani be relevant to his plan?"

"I don't know. Maybe he thought she had information. He might have had her kidnapped."

Julio closed his eyes and rubbed his face.

"We have to find her. Let's pay Mr. Grant a visit."

Lauren nodded. "I have an idea."

She walked to a cabinet and withdrew three stun guns and a package of syrettes.

"Call Floyd again. We need him."

BERNIE SAT ON a sofa in his penthouse, eating pretzels from a large bowl. The door cam interface buzzed. He took his comm from a side table, ran the app, and Lauren's face appeared on the screen.

He glared at her. "What do you want?"

She gave him a sly look, her eyes hooded and lips cocked to one side.

"Mr. Grant, I have information that might interest you."

His eyes narrowed. "And just what information is that?"

"I understand you're interested in operations on 2060RT2. Perhaps we might work out a mutually beneficial arrangement."

"What makes you think that?"

"I saw your inventory request. Jim Lawrence logged it in the record. I can get you what you need."

"And why would you do that?"

"Mr. Grant, you can help me by using your board position. I need lab funding. The tightwads aren't giving me enough resources. Approval could be a vote short of passing. You have that vote."

Bernie's eyes narrowed with intrigue.

"Let's say I'm interested, Chen. Exactly what can you get me?"

"First, I'll need to talk with Bhanupriya Oka to clear up a few things. I told her you were interested in talking with her, so you might know where she is. As soon as I touch base with her, we can move on firming up our plans."

"Did you try the Hawkington Tap Room? I told her to contact my associate. His name is Corbett. He holds court there after hours. She could be there now."

"Alright, Mr. Grant. It looks like we might have a deal. I'll get back to you."

The door display went blank, and Bernie fumbled with his comm.

"Mr. Corbett? I'm sending you a gift. Her name is Chen, Oka's supervisor. She knows where all the mine items are stored. You can deal with her as you see fit."

LAUREN EASED THE door open slightly and peered inside the Hawkington Tap Room. A few patrons sat near the bar, but the room was practically empty. In a far corner, three men sat at a table. She stepped into the room and stared at them. They saw her, and she went back out the door. They rose from the table and followed.

She walked toward the auto-cab, and when the men emerged, Julio and Floyd shot them from behind with stun guns. They collapsed onto the pavement, and Lauren injected them with tranquilizer. They dragged the three unconscious men to the auto-cab and loaded them inside.

A few minutes later, the cab pulled into the lab parking area, and Lauren directed it to a dark spot near the back door.

"Check their IDs. We want Corbett."

"Here," Floyd said, pointing to one of the men.

They carried the unconscious man inside.

CORBETT AWOKE TO find himself strapped to a table, a bright light shining in his face. He jerked his head to avoid the glare and saw Lauren gazing down at him. He tried to move his arms, but they were immobilized by thick straps. An IV dispensed a stream of yellow fluid into a vein on his left arm.

"Where am I?"

"That's not important, Mr. Corbett. What is important is that you tell us where Bhanupriya Oka is."

"I have nothing to say to you."

She turned a valve on the IV.

"That's about to change, Mr. Corbett."

17

JULIO AND LAUREN exited the auto-cab a dozen meters from Bhani's apartment. Floyd waited in the cab with the sedated thugs, who had received another dose of tranquilizer. Julio and Lauren crept up the stairs and crouched outside Bhani's door, listening. They could hear a strident, angry male voice inside.

"I'm telling you, she doesn't know!"

"I tried, but Corbett isn't picking up. You said he would be there tonight."

The man's pacing was audible outside the door.

"What should I do with her? She's seen my face."

There was a moment of silence.

"I understand. No loose ends."

Lauren entered the key code, then nudged the door open slightly. When the man walked to the refrigerator, she and Julio stepped into the apartment. They saw Bhani on the couch, bound and gagged. She looked at them and then at the man. He turned toward them. Julio's stun gun snapped, and he collapsed onto the kitchen floor. Julio strode to Bhani and freed her while Lauren inspected the other rooms. She reappeared and used her comm to call Hawkington Health and Safety.

"Hello? This is Lauren Chen of the AZ lab. We need a security team there. Meet me in the rear parking lot. We have some characters you will be interested in."

MAGDI TURNED OFF the news on his office desk display. He leaned back in his chair and rubbed his hands.

"Oh, Bernie, I own you now."

Ved inspected him with a raised eyebrow.

"Dr. El-Said, didn't your mother teach you it's unseemly to gloat?"

Magdi grinned at Ved.

"It serves that bastard right. And now I—we—can finally get rid of Board Genius. I can't believe he was stupid enough to actually go to the asteroid."

"That surprised Jim Lawrence, too, after he played that little trick with the altered inventory copy. Anyone familiar with our system knows we never leave those modules in the machines. So, how long do we let Bernie stew in home detention?"

"Long enough for us to line up the votes to kick him off the board. I want Bernie gone from AZ."

Ved worked his tablet and smiled.

"We can do better than that. Ellis Hab just filed criminal and civil charges against Bernie. Lauren has a list of other goodies guaranteed to bankrupt him. And there's a cherry on top. She informed the governing board of Bernie's condo, and it's negotiating with Yuri Karpov, a local businessman, for purchase of Bernie's penthouse."

Magdi winced. "Lauren does know how to twist the knife. And it's a damn shame Bernie will have to hire legal muscle on his own dime once he's off the board." He grinned at Ved. "Behold, Dr. Rao: technical brilliance pursuing both the betterment of humanity and justice. I like it."

"Only a cynic could attribute that to anything as low as personal malice or vindictiveness," Ved said, hiding a smirk behind his coffee cup.

Magdi gasped, his face shifting from mock horror to false piety.

"Why, Dr. Rao! I can assure you my motives are as pure as the driven snow."

He turned and punched a button on his desk comm.

"Jan, send cases of the single-malt over to Joe Leighton in Operations, Jim Lawrence in Data, and Artie Kresse at Burwell Solutions."

He turned to Ved and grinned.

"I tell you, Dr. Rao, we live in interesting times!"

"That we do, Dr. El-Said. That we do."

BERNIE'S COMM BUZZED. He picked it up and listened, then his florid face blanched sheet-white.

"Mr. Karpov, I can explain—"

"I'll be taken where? Omega Station? I don't understand—"

"Work there? But I can't, I—"

"But Omega Station is at the far edge of Gamma Sector!"

"How long? Until I've paid ... how much?"

"Mr. Karpov, that's impossible. I—"

"Yes. I understand."

Bernie dropped his comm onto the carpet. He turned, stared out the glass penthouse window into the dark Martian sky, and wept.

Epilogue

LOGAN AND AVALA came down the boarding ramp into the Hawkington transport terminal, and Rapunzel headed for the AZ lab to meet with Lauren. As they walked, Logan looked at Avala.

"Rapunzel is amazing, her improbable innocence, her calm, wise, funny personality, her brilliance. She's irreplaceable."

"She'll find her own way in Sol System, starting with Lauren's projects."

"That would be a learning experience for Lauren, too, who I gather has a rather high opinion of herself. So, what are you going to show me?"

She took his hand. "You'll see."

They walked through the dome complex to the upper level. At the end of a long corridor, Avala unlocked the door to a furnished suite. Inside, the domed ceiling and transparent walls were a gateway of the imagination to the exotic Martian landscape and evening sky. A deep-red sun was setting, and stars emerged against the black curtain of space, promising unfathomable wonders beyond. Logan stood and gazed at the distant, darkening hills and the twin moons above, Phobos and Deimos.

"I've never seen such a view."

"This is a special place."

He reached out and touched her cheek. "And you're special to me."

She moved close, and they kissed for a long time.

LOGAN AND AVALA lay side by side, gazing up through the ceiling at the infinite stellar vault. He found her hand and squeezed it.

"I never thought I'd find anyone, much less anyone like you."

She smiled and kissed him, then turned her head up toward the endless spray of stars.

"Look at all of that," he said. "In time, we'll be part of it again, stardust."

"We're part of it now."

"That endlessness and my sense of mortality trouble me." He turned toward her. "But looking at you makes it easier to face. What do you think of all this?"

"That depends. All of what?"

He pointed around the suite and out the glass wall and ceiling. "Anything. Everything. Whatever you're thinking right now at this minute."

She looked back at the stars.

"That we're infinitesimal, transitory motes drifting through an infinite universe. Our perception, awareness, and intelligence are incapable of grasping the larger reality beyond. That can be difficult to understand and to accept."

"But you do?"

"I think so. Do you?"

"I try not to dwell on it. The here and now keep me too busy with my own limitations, never mind a larger reality. I try to focus on what matters now. What do you think that is?"

"The essentials: compassion, generosity, community, companionship, and love."

"In a dream, my parents spoke of things I never heard but wanted to believe. My father said our value lies in caring for those who depend on us, the innocent and the helpless. My mother said that in time, no trace of us will remain, but that doesn't matter. What matters is we existed here, together, in this form, and that we made life better for others, and that we left the world a better place."

"Maybe Rapunzel has a theory on switching realities and continuing in another universe. I would love that."

They kissed, and as they lay there, a meteor flashed across the dusky Martian sky and was gone.

Acknowledgments

I WANT TO thank my editors, Kevin Miller and Clete Smith, whose insight, eye for detail, guidance, and professionalism made this book possible.

www.ingramcontent.com/pod-product-compliance
Lightning Source LLC
Chambersburg PA
CBHW050036180626
46810CB00002B/735